# FOREVER MORTAL

## A SHADE OF MIND
## BOOK TWO

OUTLANDERS OF THE MULTIVERSE
COLLECTION

## BY D.N. LEO

Narrative Land Publishing
Narrativeland.com

## A Shade of Mind Series
### Www.narrativeland.com/shade

1-4 Random Psychic
2-4 Forever Mortal
3-4 Elusive Beings
4-4 Imperfect Divine

 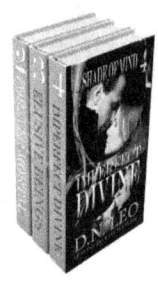  

## *Forever Mortal - A Shade of Mind - Book 2*

## Synopsis

Thirty-three years' worth of secrets fall on the shoulders of Ciaran and Madeline with a force that even their enduring love for each other might not help them survive. How much will they give, take, and sacrifice for each other and for those they love?

This second installment in an urban fantasy thriller series, filled with romance and science fiction twists and turns, will take you to the deepest corners of the minds of those who dare to love against all odds.

# CHAPTER 1

A drop of blood leaked from the center of the flower, ran down a petal, and dropped onto the wooden bench. The sound of it hitting the bench was in harmony with the raindrops tapping on the tin roof of the small shed.

Ciaran blinked.

The drop of blood vanished before his eyes.

"Ciaran!"

The voice came from Mrs. Hanson, an old gypsy, who approached him from behind. He almost jumped out of his skin. Almost. He cleared his throat, loosened up his tie and smiled. "Mrs. Hanson, I am here for the flowers."

"Certainly." Her smile was crooked. Ciaran thought she had probably been a mysterious and very beautiful woman before things had gone wrong with her alchemical practice. She had crossed the dangerous grounds of natural medicine and had paid a dear price. "I'll get the ribbons and wrap them for you."

Ciaran nodded in appreciation and returned to examine the flowers.

The purple strikes and swirls on the white petals of the Mountain Avens he had chemically engineered looked perfect. He understood why Juliette liked these wild flowers. They were plain, free, and determined, just like her spirit. He had created the purple strikes on the petals to make the flowers uniquely hers. Or maybe, to reflect her in his mind.

She had fallen in love with the flowers when they were on their honeymoon in Ireland over a year ago.

She'd intrigued him since the very first time they met. He was checking out a rare book in the library at Oxford University. She approached him, a total stranger, and asked if she could borrow a few dollars for a cup of pumpkin soup. Who could say no to her brilliant smile, magnificent flaming red hair, and eyes that contained a sea of innocence.

She did have a perfect explanation for asking. She wanted the soup. The shop was closing, so there wasn't enough time for her to run back to her dorm for the money. And after she got her soup, he walked her home to get his money back. At least, that was his excuse.

One thing led to another, and the next thing he knew, he married her despite his mother's objection.

"These flowers are cursed." Mrs. Hanson's voice interrupted Ciaran's concentration.

"I beg your pardon?" Ciaran had never raised his voice to Mrs. Hanson, or to anyone, but this statement not only demeaned his work and his belief in science but also his intentions to Juliette.

Mrs. Hanson shrugged as she wrapped a sheet of tissue paper around a pot of Mountain Avens and affixed a bow to it.

"I'm not a believer, Mrs. Hanson."

"Then you should start believing."

"You're wasting my time. What's the problem with the flowers?"

"You and Juliette are my good students. I don't want one of you to end up dead. I've been watching these flowers grow every day in my lab. They aren't normal. A couple of them turned red and bled drops of blood before they died yesterday."

"And you didn't think to let me know?"

"I'm letting you know now. You think I should have called your headquarters and wormed my way through an army of your minions just to tell you your little flowers died under tragic circumstances?"

Ciaran shrugged and pushed the pot of flowers away.

"So you don't want the flowers now? You believe me that they're cursed?"

"Of course I don't believe you. But you've said it now, and I don't feel comfortable giving them to Juliette anymore."

"Very well then. It's your decision." Mrs. Hanson smiled and turned on her heel to leave.

"Mrs. Hanson!"

"Yes."

"Never mind." Ciaran turned and strode out of Mrs. Hanson's little lab. There was no way in hell he was going to ask her whether the curse would still have an effect even if he didn't touch the flowers. *Ciaran LeBlanc is not superstitious,* he scolded himself.

He invented medicine that could change the landscape of science. He understood and accepted the fine line between science and fiction. He understood the human cognitive system and how theology worked on the human mind.

People had different beliefs. He could tolerate the differences. *But a curse? Hell no.* He wouldn't even mention it to Juliette because it was ludicrous. Juliette was a scientist.

He accidentally stepped on a bunch of wild daisies on his way out. As he moved his foot away, he saw trace of blood.

He jumped off the flowers, but the blood vanished right in front of him.

*What the hell?* He shook his head. He had been working way too hard in the last couple of weeks on a new project. It must be fatigue. Ciaran left Mrs. Hanson's house in a hurry.

He needed to go home.

# CHAPTER 2

The familiar scent of vanilla and roses greeted Ciaran. He kicked his shoes off on the lush carpet of his master suite at Mon Ciel, the palace belonging to his family.

He might tell Juliette about the blood flowers. Whether or not he believed in superstition, what happened bothered him more than a little.

He pulled the tie from his collar and walked into the closet when a cool hand covered his eyes from behind. A voice as light and colorful as an Irish lullaby whispered into his ear, "Hello, stranger. My husband won't be happy at all when he finds out about you."

He turned around. "Your husband shouldn't be surprised. He married such a beautiful woman, he should know he's got competition."

He lifted her up. Juliette wrapped her long legs around his waist and let him carry her to bed. He lay her down on the bed and ravished her mouth. He hadn't seen her all day long—he was starved for her. He could comfortably justify it as the lust of newlyweds.

His hands stopped on her flaming red gown. She was wearing artfully applied makeup and her favorite perfume.

"Is there an occasion I have forgotten?" he asked, searching his mind frantically but coming up with nothing of significance attached to this particular day.

Juliette sat up, adjusted her hair, and smiled at him. "Do you like the dress?"

"Only if you wear it . . . and then take it off when appropriate . . ." He grinned.

He stood next to the bed, preparing for whatever might be coming at him. She still lay down, lazily rubbing her bare foot against his thighs.

"You've got to have an opinion about the dress as I'm wearing it to a very important function in a couple of weeks." She smiled.

Ciaran rolled his eyes and flopped face down on the bed. Juliette rubbed his back and wrapped her long legs around him. "I don't care what your forever-extended family will do for your birthday. But I have to have my private time with you. Also you have to open my presents before you deal with everyone else."

"I'm not dealing with anyone." His voice was muffled in the mattress.

"Darling, you're turning thirty. You've got to grow up at some point."

He sat up, leaning against the headboard. "This is my room, and you are my wife. That's all I want to know right now. I don't want to bring my family or anyone else into this bedroom."

She stood up. "And that's why we're celebrating your birthday here and now, just the two of us!"

He laughed. "It's a very attractive proposition. But it would be even better if you didn't wear any dress at all."

She winked. "I've got to wear something for you to take off." She went to the wall cabinet and opened it. Inside was a tray with appetizers, a small birthday cake, champagne, and a small box wrapped in a bright purple ribbon. She poured champagne into some tall, slender glasses and brought them over to the bed.

She was stunning. He took his glass, still sitting on the bed, his eyes fixed on her face. He just wanted to ravish those lips that were made for sex. He hopped off the bed.

"No. You stay right there, birthday boy." She used a single finger to push him back to a sitting position on the bed. She climbed onto him and straddled his lap, facing him. As she gazed at him, he caught a brief glimpse of something strange in her eyes, but he was too distracted to dwell on it.

She drained her champagne. When he reached to kiss her lips, she stopped him. She yanked his shirt open and moved her lips to his chest. His pulse quickened, but just when his hands started to roam over her body, she whispered, "Let's look at your presents first." She put a small box in his hand.

He smiled and opened it. It was a small vial containing a clear liquid. He opened his mouth to say something, but she put a finger on his lips to stop his words. "You don't have to take it. But if your migraines turn bad, promise me you'll give this a try."

"Juliette!"

"Unless you don't trust me."

"You're one of the most competent engineers I've ever met. But I don't believe in Mrs. Hanson's natural medicines. I know you use her ingredients."

Juliette smiled. "I understand. And as I said, you don't have to take it."

He touched her cheek. "I don't want to disappoint you. Let's not argue over a headache medicine."

"What about something grander? Life, for example." She hummed the tune of a song she had written during their honeymoon, "Little hummingbird, do you see the sky? It is free. It is yours. Fly. Past the mountains. Past the oceans. There you will find love . . ."

"Juliette, what have you done?" He was beginning to understand the strange look in her eyes before. What he had seen was a shade of dark satisfaction. "Have you been working on the Golden Life?" he asked, knowing the answer already.

It was a project they'd started together before they got married—a medicine that could revive the newly dead. If successful, it would change the landscape of modern medicine. Only that would give Juliette this look of accomplishment.

"You have to be happy with this present, Ciaran. We've got it. We've made it. The Golden Life. I revived the lab rat. It didn't just come back as it was before—it was *better* than before death."

He had guessed the answer, but it still felt as if she had pulled the rug out from under him. "Are you out of your mind, Juliette?"

"You've worked on it your whole life, Ciaran. Why do you suddenly want to stop? Is it because it needs one ingredient you don't approve of?"

"And you've gone ahead and put it in apparently!" he could feel his rage coming. *Control*, he warned himself.

She smiled, a warm smile that was fading by the second. "You were right. That ingredient enabled the completion of the medicine. But it works. It's cruel, but it *works*, Ciaran." The smile had faded from her face, and she swayed. He caught her in his arms and carried her to the bed.

"Jesus Christ, don't tell me you tried it on yourself."

"Not yet."

"What did you take?"

She was almost out of breath. "My potion. There's nothing you can do, Ciaran. It was in my champagne glass." She smiled again.

"I can't believe you would do this to me, Juliette. Where's the damn drug?"

"In the cabinet."

He scrambled to the cabinet and saw another present dressed in purple ribbon. Opening it, he found a syringe in a box. He grabbed it and darted toward his wife.

Juliette lay in the bed, her eyes glassed over, but she still hummed her song. "Little hummingbird, do you see the sky?"

She grabbed his hand when he wanted to inject the medicine into her. "Not yet, Ciaran. If you do it now, it won't work."

"I can't wait until you die. I can't do that . . ."

"You have to. You should be happy, Ciaran, for what we have accomplished."

"I don't care . . ." He gathered her into his arms and rocked her. Regardless of whether he liked it or not, he knew she had to die for the medicine to work. She had to die so he could revive her. "Tell me you're not in pain, please . . ." he whispered.

"You were born to do this, Ciaran. You will change people's lives. You're a crusader."

"You don't know what it means to me, so don't say that."

"I know what it means to you. I know what it's like to do something that's larger than life. If I could be a part of your journey, I'll be happy."

"Please tell me you're not in pain . . ."

"I love you, Ciaran . . ." She closed her eyes and drew in her last breath.

He felt the vibration of emotion ready to burst out from him. His uncontrollable rage was coming. He was furious at himself and at the life's mission he'd set himself up with. He was angry it had caught up to the woman he loved. But there was no time to wallow in self-pity now. He held his breath and steadied his hands. He couldn't make mistakes now. He had to stay calm. He put Juliette down on the bed and checked the syringe. Then he injected the golden liquid into her.

He waited.

Ten seconds.

Thirty seconds.

Sixty seconds.

His head was pounding with a migraine, but he ignored it and concentrated on Juliette. There were no vital signs indicating she was coming back.

*Stay calm!* He stood from the bed and took the syringe. He would go to the lab, check the sample, and find the solution. He always found a way to get himself out of impossible situations. He had taken only two steps when the room exploded with light. Ciaran was thrown against the wall like a rag doll.

When he pulled himself up, he saw a man in his late fifties with flowing white hair, standing in a circle of white and blue light in the middle of the room. He looked quite formidable in his long black robe. "You killed her," said the man.

"No, I didn't. But if I don't get to the medicine, she will die."

The man looked Ciaran up and down. "I thought you were better than this. If it was possible to make the Golden Life, you would have made it."

The Golden Life was his deepest secret—only people in his family would know about it. His mind raced hundreds of possibilities why this stranger knew his secret. But he had to tend to Juliette. "I have to get to the lab!" Ciaran rushed toward the door.

An invisible force grabbed at him and threw him to the wall again. "No point. She's dead, and that's your fault."

The man stared at Ciaran. The man didn't making any physical movement except for a slight narrowing of his eyes. The invisible force squeezed around Ciaran's neck, choking him.

"Air bending. Who are you?" Ciaran gasped for air.

The man smirked. "You're knowledgeable, Ciaran, but not enough to save yourself."

The migraine was nothing compared to the pain the force was causing him right now. His life was drifting away from him. "Who . . . are . . . you?"

"Mon Ciel isn't as safe as your mother thought. All I need is a channel to get in here." The man narrowed his eyes even more, and the force squeezed harder at Ciaran's neck and crushed his body. Then Ciaran heard the door burst open. People stormed into the room. There was the sound of a gunshot and a struggle.

And then he didn't remember anything else.

## CHAPTER 3

*Seven years later.*

The phone buzzed for the third time. A news reporter on the wall screen in front of the bed was still elaborating on the death of Detective Adamson.

Madeline stared at the phone. 'No Caller ID' appeared on its small screen. "How do you know it's Stefan? It could be Jo."

On the other side of the bed, Ciaran tossed his clothes on. Madeline winced. The two bullet wounds and the five gashes on his body hadn't had a chance to heal. Not that she was one to complain about the explosive sex they'd just had—that certainly hadn't helped his recovery—but she wished they had more time to let him rest.

"If it's Jo, she'll leave a message," Ciaran said.

"Jo said she was going to your London headquarters. We don't know if she was with Adamson when Stefan killed him." She knew she was talking nonsense again. She tended to babble when she was nervous. And she had every right to be.

Ten years in journalism should have taught her better than letting herself be used by Stefan to get inside Mon Ciel. Stefan had killed Mrs. Rutherford and had shot Ciaran and Tadgh and then fled without getting what he wanted.

Stefan had arranged the kidnapping of Jo. Madeline should have anticipated what he would do when blackmailing Ciaran didn't help him obtain the information he wanted. He would kidnap Jo again. *Damn it!* Madeline cursed to herself.

"If he hasn't had a chance to talk to me, he won't get to demand anything. He will keep Jo alive because she's his currency now, am I right?" she asked Ciaran again, more to reassure herself that she was doing the right thing.

Ciaran headed toward the door, and she trailed behind him. He said nothing but headed down the hall toward the old section of Mon Ciel. The phone in Madeline's hand had stopped buzzing.

Ciaran stopped in front of a double-doored room. The rusty handles suggested it hadn't had visitors for a while. He gazed briefly at the handles. A flash of pain crossed his eyes, so quickly that Madeline didn't notice.

Ciaran cleared his throat, a tell-tale sign that he was about to say something difficult for him. "This used to be my room," Ciaran said and shoved his hands in his pockets.

She nodded and waited patiently for the next bit of information.

"Juliette died in here. I left Mon Ciel after that incident. The room—the whole place, in fact—was deserted after that. We still have maintenance staff. But the family rarely comes back here."

She pulled one of his hands from his pocket and rubbed her thumb in his palm. She didn't know when or why she had developed that habit, but she often did it to herself whenever she needed to stay calm. She hadn't realized she was doing it to Ciaran, but by the time she noticed, it was too late. He was watching her gesture with a twinkle in his eyes.

"If the memories are too painful, why dig them up? What are you looking for here, Ciaran?"

She pulled her hand away. But he grabbed it and held on for a short moment before giving it a slight squeeze. Then he sighed and let her hand go.

"There are two places in the house that Stefan didn't search. One is this room, and the other is the old lab. He believed Juliette hid the crucifix in a statue, which suggests she didn't tell him much."

Ciaran turned, facing her now. "Before we enter this room, I need to tell you something."

He proceeded to tell her about the incident in which Juliette died.

"I didn't return to the room afterward. Mother told me it hadn't been cleaned up because she thought I wouldn't care for that. What I'm looking for in the room is a trace of the air bender. He had some kind of connection to Juliette. Maybe he controlled her in some way to learn our family secrets. He might be controlling Stefan now. If we can trace him, we'll have the upper hand when we talk to Stefan."

Madeline nodded. "I didn't realize Stefan had anything to do with aliens. Not that I know anything about him . . ."

Ciaran smiled. "An air bender doesn't necessarily have anything to do with extraterrestrials. It could be some kind of an earthly talent."

Madeline scowled. "I feel so stupid."

"Don't. It would be strange for you to know about these sort of things." Ciaran chuckled. "I know because it's my field of interest, and I research the topic quite extensively."

"I know, but it still doesn't make me feel any less stupid."

"Humm. How about this explanation? It has to do with dimensions. You know our standard three-dimensional world."

"Yes—vertical, horizontal, depth. And time is another dimension, I hear." She grinned.

"You see, you're not too bad after all. Anything with a status of being that changes constitutes a dimension. Our mind is a dimension, for example."

"Like we are changing our minds all the time?"

Ciaran laughed. "No. That's an ingrained human psychological problem. Status of mind is more like a perception of the world in general. Let's say you believe this world is heaven, and you behave accordingly. That's your status of mind. When that status changes, it constitutes a dimension."

"Okay. I get it."

"There are people who have the ability to influence other people's status of mind. They can use their talent to manipulate people and drive their behavior."

"Like hypnotizing people?"

Ciaran shook his head. "I'd call people with that talent mind benders. They can change your mind's dimension by simply wanting you to do so. They can *see* your mind."

"See it?"

"Yes. If it's their talent, the minds of others become tangible to them. They manipulate it however they want, just like you steer a car. The same deal with the air bender. He can *see* the air and manipulate it. That man turned the air into hands, and it did whatever he wanted it to do. It almost strangled me."

Madeline nodded, thinking about her psychic blue dots. "Are there many like that around?"

"I don't know, Madeline. But this air bender had a light circle around him . . ." He shook his head. "I haven't given it much thought. I didn't know much back then, but maybe the light circle was a holocast."

"A what?"

"It's like a broadcast of a hologram"

"Like in *Star Wars*?"

Ciaran chuckled. "Not quite. But yes, I can accept that explanation for now. Anyway, I think we have enough information to go inside the room."

She nodded. She wasn't nervous or anything, but Ciaran wrapped his arm around her protectively and pushed the doors open.

*Holy cow!* That was all she could think of. She froze.

# CHAPTER 4

Thousands of glaring, bright, blinking blue dots flooded the room. They hovered and swayed like waves in the ocean. They hummed. *"Little hummingbird, do you see the sky . . . ?"*

The dusty room swiveled and swung back and forth, zooming in and then back out again.

The dots kept humming. *". . . It is free. It is yours. Fly. Past the mountains. Past the oceans . . ."* Madeline's vision blurred with the glare of the blue shade.

*". . . There. You will find love . . ."*

She couldn't get a word past her mouth. She just wanted to tell Ciaran she saw the blue dots and they were singing to her.

"Madeline!"

She heard Ciaran calling out for her. But then she was flying. She tried to regain her footing, but she kept flying.

When the world stopped spinning, she realized that Ciaran was carrying her. They were at the far end of the hall, almost out of the old quarter of the house.

"Put me down, Ciaran."

He stopped walking and set her on her feet but still held on to her shoulders firmly.

"I'm okay."

"You fainted, Madeline. That's not okay. Was it because you spent a couple of nights down at the creek?" He put his hand on her forehead. "You don't have a fever."

He gazed at her, searching for an answer. The worry in those intense gray eyes bothered her. Should she tell him? After all, he'd just told her a secret that he had refused to revisit for many years.

*Hell, forget this!* "Please don't think I'm crazy, Ciaran," she began. "I don't have any magical talent. But I do see things. It's very random. I don't have a theory of what it is that I can and can't see, or even what I'm going to see. Sometimes I hear things. But most of the time, I just feel things."

He pulled her into his arms and kissed her. She didn't think romance was the reason for the kiss, rather that it was the only way he could stop her from ranting. She was babbling nonsense again, and she knew it. But then nothing was making sense to her at the moment.

When he finished with the kiss, he spoke gently, "Now, tell me one thing at a time, Madeline. What do you think you can see sometimes, and what did you see in that room?"

She drew in a breath. "I think I can see people's thoughts. They appear as blue dots. I don't know their meaning—they just hover in front of me. That's how I found you at the creek. You thought of me, and I followed the blue dots, the trail of your thoughts."

Ciaran lifted her chin up and looked into her eyes. His intense gray eyes filled with curiosity and his face lit up with fascination. "You're a . . ."

"Don't label me, Ciaran. I'm not one of your science projects." She turned around and walked away. He grabbed her elbow to stop her.

"I'm sorry. I'll never do it again. Please calm down. Stefan will ring again at any time. We should try to see if we can do something to prepare."

She stopped walking. He was right. "I'm sorry. My head just scrambled a bit. Let's get back to the room," she said.

"Not until I'm sure you'll be okay. Tell me what you saw in the room?"

"Lots of blue dots." She looked straight into his eyes. "I don't think you want to hear this, but if what I saw were thoughts, they had to be Juliette's."

"Only living people have thoughts, Madeline."

"Well, it can't be the air bender because I haven't met him. But I do have a connection with Juliette via you."

"It's not possible."

"Now you think I hallucinated it?"

"No . . ."

"When you brought me here the first night, as soon as I walked into the house, I not only saw the blue dots heading toward the old quarter, but I heard a woman's voice welcoming you home."

Ciaran raked his hands through his hair. "Juliette died in my arms. I wish it were a mistake. But it wasn't . . ."

"Does she have an Irish accent?"

Ciaran simply stared at her.

Madeline hummed the tune. *"Little hummingbird, do you see the sky . . ."*

Ciaran gestured for silence. He braced his hands on the wall. She couldn't see his face, but she guessed he was wanting to bang his head against that wall. She must have gotten it right.

He hadn't told her anything about Juliette apart from what had happened in that room, and he certainly had never mentioned her accent. And the song did it. It was Juliette's song.

"Ciaran, you asked me what I saw . . ."

"Yes, I know. I'm sorry. It was just . . ." He turned around. "Okay. Let's just go back to the room. We'll figure out what's what later. But you have to let me know right away if you feel uneasy."

She nodded and headed toward the room. When they entered again, there were no more blue dots.

*Damn!*

The room was a mess as a result of what appeared to have been a massive fight, and nobody had cleaned up a thing. Ciaran glanced at the bed and then focused on the floor in front of it. He deliberately avoided looking at Madeline. She knew he was trying to control his emotions and didn't want to create any awkward moments, so she kept silent.

He crouched and pointed to the floor. "You see the circle here? This is where the light circle landed. It must have scarred the wood . . ."

"Ciaran!"

He traced his fingers on the floor in circles.

"Ciaran!"

"Yes?" He looked up.

"I don't see any circle marks on the floor."

"You can't see these?" He pointed.

"No."

He frowned.

Then she saw a single lonely blue dot blinking in the corner of the room. She pulled at Ciaran's sleeve and nodded her head in the direction of the dot. Ciaran looked and obviously saw nothing except a sturdy cabinet standing there.

"Over there?" He pointed.

She nodded and felt a chill run up and down her spine. The air seemed to have become hollow. She heard the voice of the woman again but couldn't make sense of what she was saying. It was more like weeping or chanting of some sort.

Madeline stood up and saw Ciaran examining the cabinet without any hope of finding anything. The temperature in the room seemed to suddenly drop several degrees. She was trying to tell Ciaran to get out, but she had a feeling if she spoke, he wouldn't be able to hear her. It seemed as if they were in two different worlds.

The weeping sound still echoed in her mind.

Ciaran approached her and looked at her face. He said something, but she couldn't quite hear him. He seemed to know she was in trouble. He held her shoulder gently. And then reality suddenly blasted back at them.

"Ciaran!" a voice came from behind them.

Madeline and Ciaran both jumped out of their skin. Ciaran turned toward the voice and saw Tadgh standing at the door.

"Don't you knock?" Ciaran growled.

Tadgh raised an eyebrow. "This isn't your room anymore. Why do I need to knock? What are you two doing in here? Doctor Thomas asked for you. He wants to check up on you. Your painkillers are running out soon."

Ciaran glanced around one last time then led Madeline out of the room. "Where's Mother?" Ciaran asked Tadgh.

"I have no idea. She doesn't usually report her whereabouts to me. And after last night, I don't think she's ever told us anything real."

"What do you mean?" Ciaran asked.

"How do you think we got you back home?"

Ciaran shrugged. "I haven't thought about it. We've been busy!"

"I see." Tadgh shot a glance at Madeline and rolled his eyes. "You put Mon Ciel on lockdown, remember? She unlocked the shield. We got you onto a chopper."

Ciaran stared at Tadgh for a moment then strode down the hallway. Madeline trailed right behind. "There are only two people who have the key, and she isn't one of them. Mother didn't unlock it by herself."

"You mean Father helped her?" Tadgh asked.

"I don't want to hear about two ghosts in one day, Tadgh!" Ciaran growled and punched a code into the security pad of a room that looked like some kind of control room.

Ciaran's phone buzzed. A text message read, "Meet at British museum in one hour." The caller ID was Sciphil Two.

"What that hell is Sciphil Two?" Tadgh asked. Ciaran shook his head. At the same time, Madeline's phone buzzed.

"It's the same No Caller ID," she said, looking at Ciaran.

Ciaran nodded. She picked up the phone. From the other end of the line came Jo's voice. "Madeline?"

"Oh my God, Jo, are you okay? Where are you now?"

"I'm fine. I ran. Stephen—no Stefan—got me, but I ran."

"Where are you now?"

"In London . . . where are you?"

"Can you find your way to the British museum? We'll be there in an hour."

"I'll be there. I never get lost in a big city, and I always find you." Jo hung up.

Madeline stared at Ciaran and Tadgh.

"What's the matter?" Ciaran asked.

"I'm so sorry."

"Why? Didn't you just talk to Jo? She escaped? Why isn't that good?" Tadgh asked.

"You don't think Jo ran again, Madeline?" Ciaran asked.

She shook her head. "I'm so sorry. I think I've just given Stefan our location in the next hour. Jo makes fun of people who use the words *never* and *always*. She wouldn't say *always* with an emphasis. I didn't catch it when we spoke. I'm sorry."

"It's okay, Madeline. Stefan will be at the museum. We'll get him and bring Jo back," Ciaran said. But she caught the way he glanced at Tadgh. His eyes were too dark—they scared her.

# CHAPTER 5

The British museum looked exactly the same as Madeline found it the week before. Groups of tourists were scattered around. It was an awfully busy place for a secret meeting with the person called Sciphil Two. Perhaps it wasn't a secret meeting at all.

She caught sight of Ciaran nodding at Tadgh. Tadgh responded with a wink and patted his pocket.

"Jesus Christ, are you carrying guns?" Madeline spoke between her teeth.

Ciaran smiled. "I like to refer to them as weapons. Guns sound too primitive."

"You can't have them here! This is a museum!"

"Says who?" Tadgh asked.

"We won't use them unless absolutely necessary. I don't care to be at a disadvantage when we don't know who we're dealing with," Ciaran said.

They walked further into the ancient history section. Ciaran checked his phone and found no messages.

Suddenly, the air seemed to stop flowing. Their hearts skipped a beat. Everyone else in the museum seemed to be oblivious to it. Madeline, Ciaran, and Tadgh seemed to be in a different world—a very quiet one. They could hear their own heartbeats.

"John Dee's glass! Look!" Madeline pointed toward a display of a golden plate. As they walked closer, the air around them seemed to thicken.

Ciaran grabbed Madeline and Tadgh to stop their movement toward the display. Ciaran asked them, "You hear anything strange? Like an echo in the air?" Ciaran shook his head as if shaking away the noise in his ears.

"No, I just feel strange, like the air is thick as gel and lacking in oxygen," Madeline said.

"It feels like the air has been vacuumed out of the room to me," Tadgh said.

Ciaran approached the glass cabinet of John Dee's exhibit with caution. The thick air seemed to follow him. Ciaran spoke to no one in particular. "We haven't the time nor inclination to play hide and seek. Show yourself, or we'll leave."

In the air right in front of them, a white and blue beam flashed straight to the plate. The light bounced back from it, forming a cone shape in which text appeared. *"Hello,"* it said.

"This is a very primitive model of the hologame technology," Ciaran said.

*"Yes,"* the text printed.

"Can we talk elsewhere if all you need is a shiny plate to reflect your light on? What if people walk in and see?" Madeline asked.

*"Other people's vision in the same space with you has been blocked. You are fine where you stand. The plate reflects the correct frequency,"* the text read.

"What do you want?" Ciaran asked.

*"We need to warn you that the LeBlancs are in danger."*

"Who are you, and what sort of danger are we facing?" asked Ciaran.

*"We are your council and your guards when your position is active. At the moment, we can only alert you of possible danger. The danger is coming. It's time . . ."* The text flickered, faded away, flickered again, and then was totally gone.

"What position?" Ciaran asked.

"Damn it. That wasn't very helpful," Tadgh snarled at the air.

Ciaran grunted in pain and held his ears. A drop of blood trickled from his nose. Madeline tried to hold him steady as he swayed. When Tadgh approached to help, Ciaran said, "Time me." And then he fell to the floor, unconscious.

Madeline shook his shoulders and got no response.

"Tadgh!" she called out.

Tadgh stood frozen. He shoved his hands in his pockets, looking as if he was somewhere else. Madeline shook Ciaran's shoulders again. "Come on, you're scaring me." Then she looked up as Stefan walked into the room with Jo at his side. He had his arm around Jo's waist. Madeline knew that underneath Jo's jacket, Stefan was holding a weapon to her.

"Tadgh!" she called out, but the only difference between he and Ciaran was that Ciaran was on the floor and Tadgh still stood, looking like a statue. The text had said that other people couldn't see them. That was the hope Madeline held on to.

Stefan glanced around the room. Jo did the same.

"Nobody's here. Let's go," Jo said.

Madeline caught an unusual sign in Jo's eyes. Jo saw something, Madeline thought.

"Be quiet. If you can decode my sister's disk, I don't need Ciaran. I shot at him before, so I can't just come back and ask him nicely. But you can use your charm to get what we need," Stefan told Jo.

On the floor, Ciaran stirred and opened his eyes. Tadgh immediately switched back to reality. Madeline helped Ciaran sit up. "How long was I out?" he asked Tadgh.

"Precisely thirty-three seconds."

She could see Tadgh wore no watch and had nothing with which to track the time.

Ciaran saw Stefan and Jo now. So did Tadgh. Tadgh growled and turned to walk toward Stefan, his hand ready on his pocket. Ciaran grabbed at Tadgh.

"Wait. I can't fight yet. I don't think they can see or hear us." Ciaran stood up.

Jo gazed straight in their direction.

"Are you sure they can't see or hear us?" Tadgh asked.

"Jo has very good instincts. She might be able to feel us," Madeline said.

Stefan steered Jo in their direction, keeping his hand on her back.

"He has a knife on her," Ciaran said. Both Ciaran and Tadgh had their hands in their pockets. Ciaran moved Madeline behind him.

"Are they going to bump into us?" Madeline asked.

"I'm not sure what will happen," Ciaran said.

Jo gazed in their direction and stopped walking. "I need to go, Stefan."

Stefan stopped on his tracks. "Go where?"

"The girl's room. You can come with me if you like."

"Don't fuck around with me, Jo. You stay right here. They'll turn up sooner or later unless you gave them a hint over the phone." Stefan glared at Jo.

"Look, Stefan, I want to go home. I told you I can decode the disk for you. You don't have to wait for them."

"What are they saying?" Tadgh asked.

"Can't you hear them?" Madeline asked.

Tadgh shook his head.

"Can you, Madeline?" Ciaran asked.

Madeline nodded.

"You tried for hours, and you've got nothing," Stefan raised his voice.

"If you knew a scrap of computer programming, you would know it takes an awful lot of time to decode a program at that level. I could have been faster if you'd put me in a habitable place. Not that dingy little hole in the wall you call a house. And if you'd pulled down those silly distracting bells on the veranda, stopped the flutes in the garden, and let me work in the actual house rather than a basement . . ."

"Lower your voice or I'll hurt you," Stefan growled. Jo stiffened. Stefan must have pushed his knife harder into her back.

"Coward," Tadgh snarled and moved forward. Ciaran grabbed at him, pulling him back.

"I can take him. I'm a good shot. I'll blow his brains out before he even knows what hit him," Tadgh said.

"Do you know how long it takes to slit someone's throat, Tadgh? One second. He's closer to Jo than you are. You haven't seen what Stefan is capable of. He blew a man's head off without a thought."

Tadgh shoved Ciaran away from him.

"As long as Jo behaves, he won't hurt her," Ciaran continued. "What did Jo just say, Madeline?"

She repeated it to Ciaran. "She must sense someone is listening. She's giving us the location of the house."

Ciaran nodded. "And I know exactly where it is."

Stefan seemed convinced that there was no point in waiting for Ciaran. He took Jo out of the room.

The text flicked and appeared in front of them again. *"Your enemies are attempting to obtain our frequency. If they can get to us, they can get to you. The disk contains the frequency."* A number appeared—a countdown from five seconds.

*Five. Four. Three. Two. One.*

Ciaran grabbed at Madeline and Tadgh, pulling them back toward the far end of the room. The air stretched, following them like a rubber band.

# CHAPTER 6

If Madeline wasn't mistaken, they were exceeding the speed limit on the highway. From behind the steering wheel, Ciaran gazed at the road ahead of him. He didn't look as if he wanted to talk, but she asked anyway.

"Did you expect an explosion from the five-second countdown at the museum?"

"Better to be safe than sorry. We don't know who Sciphil Two is yet," Ciaran warned,

"I still feel sorry for those visitors. We appeared in front of them out of nowhere. They must have gotten the fright of their lives," Tadgh said.

"I guess we would be sorrier if it had been an actual explosion." Madeline smiled.

Ciaran didn't say anything further. *Mind reading would be a handy talent to have right now,* Madeline thought. She'd love to get inside his head and know what he was thinking about.

"Where are we going?" she asked.

"Mortlake. Mrs. Hanson's house. You've been there," Ciaran said.

"I don't care where we're going as long as I arrive with all of my organs intact," Tadgh blurted from the back seat. Madeline turned around and saw beads of sweat running down his forehead.

"Have I ever gotten you into a car accident, Tadgh?" Ciaran asked.

"I don't want you to break your record, Ciaran. Slow down, will you?"

"Madeline isn't complaining. Neither should you."

"How can you be so sure Jo was talking about Mrs. Hanson's house?" she asked.

"I spent a lot of time in the part of the house she described. The bells, the flutes, the basement underneath the kitchen. It has to be her place."

"Ciaran studied flowers there for years," Tadgh added.

"It was natural medicine, not flowers. And I consulted with her. I didn't study anything with her,"

Ciaran snarled. His voice and his eyes were disturbingly cold. He reached over, touched Madeline's hand. He felt her brace herself, and he slammed on the brakes then stomped on the accelerator. The movements threw Tadgh sideways and back.

"Hey! I know you're a tough guy, you don't have to prove it. If you're mad about the number thirty-three, it isn't my fault. You asked me to time you!" Tadgh yelled.

"You know nothing about it, Tadgh. Let it be."

"I don't know much. But I can always ask Mother. I'm sure she knows. Just like the way she knows how to unlock Mon Ciel's shield that you think is invincible."

"Leave her out of this."

"The hell I will. Sciphil Two, whoever that was, said our family is in trouble. You don't have the right to speak for all of us, Ciaran. Not only I am talking to Mother, I'm going to talk to everyone in the family."

Ciaran swung the car over to the emergency shoulder of the highway and stopped. "Get out," he said.

"You don't get to kick everyone out of your life at your leisure, Ciaran."

"It's my car that I'm kicking you out of. Get out before I cause you bodily damage."

Madeline turned around and looked at Tadgh, while Ciaran stared at him from the reflective mirror. Tadgh put on a stern face and sat unmoving.

Ciaran slammed the heel of one hand on the steering wheel and got out of the car. He strode along the shoulder of highway. Madeline got out and went after him.

"Ciaran, talk to me, please. What's happening?"

"You don't have to worry about this. I don't want you to get tangled up in my mess."

"As far as I'm concerned, I don't have a choice. I know you and your family have a lot going on, but I brought Stefan into your home, and it seemed to stir up a lot of dust from the past. But I have my friend to save, and whether I like it or not, I'm a part of this mess now."

Ciaran looked away. She grabbed him and spun him around to face her. "Please. Tell me."

"I just recalled now—the air bender said the thirty-three year cycle would come. He said I broke his family, and he will break mine."

"How did you remember it just now but not before? Are you sure the memories are there, or did one of those talented mind benders you told me about put them in your head?"

He looked at her in surprise. "You're very good Madeline. Not everyone catches on to the idea so easily."

"It comes with the job. I've seen enough weird things." She touched his face gently, the face God had created when he was in a very good mood. "If you feel anything, just tell me. A man is allowed to have emotions, Ciaran. You can be out there, saving the world, being a crusader, changing people's lives. But once in a while, when you just need to talk, I'll listen."

He nodded. "The information must be in my subconscious. He said that after I'd passed out. I didn't remember it before because the triggers weren't strong enough, and I don't think I wanted to remember." He held her hands. "I still don't know how the thirty-three year cycle resonates with my family's affairs. But the man came back because he thought I had killed Juliette, and that Juliette was the cause of all this, so I am responsible for what happens to my family."

"I have to agree with Tadgh on this point. You can't take all the responsibility. And kicking everyone out of your life isn't a very good way to deal with it."

"My family is vulnerable now. I don't know what will come for us or how to deal with it." Ciaran turned to look at Tadgh, who was stepping out of the car.

"But as you said, I'm in this with you. Whatever it is, you won't deal with it alone—like it or not." She smiled at him.

He tilted her face up, rubbing his thumb over the dimple on her left cheek. "When you said you'd take care of me, you meant it!"

"I'm in it for the long haul."

"And you'll let me do the same for you?"

She nodded.

"You promise to tell me everything? I've told you everything I know. But I don't know anything about you, Madeline."

"Didn't you say you have access to one of the most secretive and powerful databases on Earth?" She chucked.

"The things I want to know are not in the database."

She tucked a strand of stray hair away, tiptoed, and kissed him.

"Promise me?" he asked again.

She smiled and nodded. Then he kissed her as if it was the first time they'd ever kissed. He hands gripped at the dip in her back and her neck, lifting her off the ground.

"I don't have all day. We have places to be!" Tadgh tapped the side of the car.

Ciaran ended the kiss and chuckled. He walked back toward the car. "All right, you don't have to hurt my car. We're leaving."

As she began to walk toward the car, Madeline saw a handful of blue dots at the corner of her eyes. A chill shot up through her spine and numbed her brain. The dots weren't hovering like they usually did, but they stayed fixed on the road, forming the number thirty-three. Some of them weren't the usual haunting blue color but were instead a grainy blood red .

"Go away. I have nothing to do with this," she scolded. The dots stared back silently at her.

"I have no idea what thirty-three means," she said. She looked toward the car and saw Ciaran had climbed in behind the steering wheel.

The dots flashed at her. Flashed. Flashed. Flashed. Then disappeared.

She glared at the road where the dots had been one last time before turning on her heel and heading back to the car. Suddenly a pain stabbed at her heart as an old emotional wound just broke open and started bleeding.

She might know what thirty-three meant. She hoped she was wrong. But if not, she might have to let go of the relationship she had just found with Ciaran.

# CHAPTER 7

Just before dusk, Ciaran, Madeline, and Tadgh arrived at Mrs Hanson's house. Ciaran parked a block away. As they approached the house, they could see Stefan driving away with Jo in the passenger seat.

"We missed them again," Madeline muttered.

"They might come back," Ciaran said. "We should take the opportunity to see what he's got set up inside."

They neared the front of the house. The police had sealed the place up after clearing away Mrs. Hanson's body.

"How on Earth did he get in here with the police seal intact?" Tadgh asked, looking at the front door.

"He's a cop himself. Don't you think he could figure that out?" Madeline asked somewhat sarcastically.

Ciaran said nothing but moved directly to the back of the house. The back door wasn't sealed but locked by an old padlock on a rusty handle. Tadgh chuckled. "Apparently, the cops didn't think this was a major crime scene." Tadgh pulled out his pocket knife to work on the lock.

"No need to do that," Ciaran said and walked toward the side of the house. He opened a small window, gestured for Tadgh and Madeline to stay back and hopped inside.

Moving to the living room, Ciaran scanned the area. Everything looked the same. He had spent a considerable amount of time here with Juliette. It was all too familiar, and he didn't care for it.

What had happened in the last couple of weeks had turned an old emotional scar into an open wound— fresh, raw, and bleeding. The wound had never really healed, and it now needed his attention.

He came back to the window and reached out a hand to help Madeline in. "No one else is here," Ciaran said. "Stefan wouldn't rig this place or lay traps. He only needed a place to stay, and the cops would be all over him."

"How do the police know?" Madeline asked.

"I asked Lindsay to give the police an anonymous tip," Ciaran answered as he moved to the kitchen that could barely accommodate three people.

The flutes hanging from the trees in the garden and the bells dangling on the veranda composed strange melodies, and the haunting sounds poured into the room from the window.

Ciaran approached a small cabinet that looked as if it would crumble into pieces if he opened its door too quickly. Inside were rows of ceramic cups and plates and a teapot. He grabbed the teapot handle and turned slightly. The dining table slid aside to reveal a rickety wooden staircase that led to the basement.

Tadgh grabbed Ciaran and Madeline, pulling them backward. "If someone's hiding down there, we'll be shot in places we won't much care for."

"You're not going down there, Tadgh. I am. You stay here and keep watch in case Stefan comes back."

"You always get to do the fun bit," Tadgh muttered and sat down on a chair at the kitchen table.

"Don't touch anything," Ciaran said as he started to descend a small set of stairs. Madeline followed.

The basement was spacious. It looked like the entire house was built on top of it. It wasn't a lab—there were no vials, jars, or chemical compounds of any kind. The room was almost empty with a large rectangular table in one corner and projector-like equipment hanging from all four corners.

There were shiny panels that looked like black mirrors lining the walls, angled in no particular logical order. Some of the panels were shattered, and an apparently damaged projector dangled from the ceiling.

"This is a holocast room, a primitive model," Ciaran said. "Stefan must have taken the control center with him. Without it, I can't make any sense of the setup here. Especially, this . . ." Ciaran pointed toward a round reflective plate sitting in a corner. "I don't know what that does."

"It looks like John Dee's glass, the one we saw at the museum," Madeline commented. She looked at the round plate but didn't touch it. There were no cords or electrical connections of any kind attached to the object. "Could it simply be an artifact? A symbol, or some kind of worship thing?" Madeline suggested.

"It's a communication center. One that gathers channels, frequency and connections of different dimensions. But what we have here is too primitive to do anything like that."

"You means this room can facilitate communication between extraterrestrial agents?"

Ciaran nodded. "Very likely."

Madeline sneered. "I can't imagine a ninety-year-old gypsy handling this technology."

"It's not her, Madeline. We talked about this. What we met here wasn't her."

"Right. You said they rewired her brain. It was a robot lookalike."

He couldn't help but chuckle. Madeline always had a very interesting way of interpret things. Sometimes her interpretation was simple and basic, but most of the time, it was frighteningly relevant to the core of the matter. He wondered if it was the quality of a good journalist or simply her unique intuition.

"You said on the bridge there were two groups of people—or robot lookalikes—fighting. One group was on your side, and the other was on Stefan's. Before Stefan revealed his intention to get inside Mon Ciel, he was on my side. Mrs. Hanson wanted to kill me, so she couldn't possibly be my friend. And now Stefan is using her house. So who are our friends and who are our foes here, Ciaran?"

"Stefan may be on the side of the people who neurologically killed Mrs. Hanson—or rewired her brain, in your terms. That was why he knew this place. He may have manipulated Mrs. Hanson to send you to Fosse Way to intentionally put you in danger so that you would call for his help."

"But he got lucky, I got you in the process."

Ciaran smiled. "Yes, it was lucky that he was able to skip a couple of steps to get inside Mon Ciel. But even if he hadn't, he would have found another way and put you in further danger."

She stared at him in a way that let Ciaran know she was about to ask an important question. "What's in the crucifix, Ciaran? Why would Stefan kill to get it?"

"A powerful spell that would cause an apocalypse." Tadgh stuck his head down from the top of the stairs and grinned. "Okay, okay. I know that's lame. But come on, if there's nothing useful down there, we'd better leave."

Madeline raised an eyebrow, looking at Ciaran.

"I'll tell you about it later. Not about Tadgh's flawed theory about the spell and the apocalypse, but about what I think Stefan is looking for in the crucifix. Let's go," Ciaran said and climbed back up the stairs. His head was pounding now. In the rush of the morning's events, he had forgotten to take his painkillers. Now the bullets and stab wounds were punishing him for it.

There was the sound of silenced guns shooting at the shelves in the kitchen, and cups and plate in the opened cabinet came crashing to the floor. Ciaran flew up from the basement.

"Tadgh!" he called out.

# CHAPTER 8

Ciaran saw Tadgh's shadow chasing someone outside in the garden. He glanced at the damage the bullets had wreaked on the kitchen furniture. If Tadgh hadn't been quick, the consequences could have been unimaginable.

Madeline and Ciaran heard a crash from the shed where Mrs. Hanson had kept her botanical lab to make natural medicines. Ciaran pushed Madeline behind him as they approached and held his gun tightly. They approached the shed slowly. Ciaran pointed his gun at the lock on the door and fired. Ciaran pushed the door open little by little.

All was quiet inside the shed. Ciaran pushed the door open a bit wider. A furry black shadow leaped through the gap and landed outside. Ciaran aimed, ready to shoot. In front of Ciaran and Madeline was an enormous black cat, nearly the size of a small leopard. The cat blinked its bright yellow eyes and darted at Ciaran.

"Be careful!" Madeline squealed.

"Don't worry. This is Migi. She's very gentle."

Migi meowed and waved her tail contentedly as she rubbed against Ciaran's legs.

"Oh my God, there are two tails," Madeline gasped.

Ciaran chuckled. "She originally had only one tail, and she was a very tiny kitten. Mrs. Hanson manipulated her appearance using her magic and natural medicine." Ciaran patted and scratched the cat below the jaw and elicited a loud purring. "So Migi became quite big and very intelligent, but she still doesn't speak, I'm afraid."

Madeline reached her hand out nervously.

"She doesn't bite," Ciaran said.

"Just in case she changes her mind, I'd like to keep my fingers," she said, curling her fingers into her fist.

Migi licked Madeline's hand and rubbed her head against it.

"Among other things, I didn't approve of Mrs. Hanson's practice on animals. Her alchemical practice was so distorted that often she turned transmutation into mutilation."

"Transmutation?"

"It's an alchemical term. The less you know, the better, Madeline." The cat came back to rub at Ciaran's legs.

"Who's feeding her now?" Madeline asked.

"I don't know. I think she's very self-sufficient."

They heard footsteps, and then Tadgh appeared, pushing a man in front of him. Tadgh kept his gun pressed to the man's back.

"He won't say a word," Tadgh said. "Do you have any special mouth-opening techniques, Madeline? We boys only have our fists."

The man's eyes were bizarre—a feline green.

"Who are you?" Ciaran asked. The man stared at him but made no move to answer. Ciaran circled the man, observing him. He had seen these eyes before. He remembered now, on the bridge, the robot who had shielded him from the bullets. Its eyes had flashed the same bright green shade before it shut down.

If his speculation was correct, these robots didn't appear to have high levels of problem-solving abilities. They were merely soldier robots. That was why they couldn't get him to talk.

"Did Sciphil Two send you?"

The man nodded.

"Oh, so he can understand simple questions," Tadgh said.

"It's a robot, Tadgh. Very low level. Not programmed to do anything complicated," Ciaran explained to his brother.

"But it shot at me. Is killing such a simple task?" Tadgh muttered.

"Your mission is to kill Stefan?" Ciaran asked.

No response.

"It probably wouldn't know Stefan or Stephen," Madeline said.

"Your mission is to target residents of this house?" Ciaran asked.

The man nodded.

Tadgh rolled his eyes. "This is ridiculous. Now we have to speak robot?"

Suddenly Migi stepped out from the darkness and hissed. Tadgh jumped and pointed his gun.

"No, no . . . it's a cat. Don't shoot, Tadgh!" Ciaran yelled.

"Fuck me, it's a *hell* of a cat!" Tadgh grumbled and glared at the animal.

Migi kept hissing at the air, her tails waving frantically in different directions.

They heard a faint movement in the air, but before they could make sense of it, the man they had captured flew at Ciaran, pressing him to the ground. Two small darts appeared on the man's back, and Tadgh shot in the direction of a shadow in the bush and gave chase.

Ciaran pushed the robot off of him. The man's eyes filmed over instantly, and his body started to melt, turning into yellow liquid. The liquid pooled on the grass, smoking and sending the stench of burning flesh into the air. Then the liquid evaporated and, except for a burned patch on the grass, there was no sign of the dead man.

Madeline helped Ciaran stand up. "You're burning up, Ciaran."

"I'm running out of painkillers."

Tadgh returned, puffing. "Lost him." Then he saw the patch on the grass. "Where did he go?"

"He evaporated," Madeline said.

"Look out!" Ciaran flew at Tadgh, shooting at a shadow on the way down. A dart stuck into a wood panel behind Tadgh. The three of them rushed to the side of the garden where they saw the shadow drop after Ciaran's shot.

A man lay on the ground, looking up at them. He said nothing but pulled out a small dart.

"Stop!" Ciaran yelled and grabbed the man's hand. The man struggled and waved the point of the dart dangerously close to Ciaran's hand.

Madeline grabbed Ciaran from behind, pulling him off the man. "Let him go, Ciaran." They both fell backward onto the ground.

The man took the opportunity to stab the dart into his heart before he could be questioned. Like had happened before, this man evaporated into thin air.

"What's with this place? A two-tailed cat, and now evaporating men. Will we see the dragons next?" Tadgh mumbled.

"We should go before more of them show up. The robots, not the dragons," Ciaran said. He stood and helped Madeline to her feet.

"Thanks. I shouldn't have hung on to a robot programmed to self-destruct when caught," Ciaran said.

"You're welcome. I make it my life's mission to keep you alive." She grinned and kissed him lightly.

"Likewise," Ciaran said. Before they left, he turned and flicked his fingers at Migi. "Come on. You too."

"You're kidding me," Tadgh protested.

"I didn't know you were allergic to cats," Ciaran said.

"People are allergic to anesthesia. I simply don't like cats. It's a matter of choice."

"Come on, Tadgh. She's a nice and gentle cat," Madeline said.

Tadgh rolled his eyes. "Look at the size of her. I'd feel safer with TJ."

"TJ is a puppy, Tadgh. Don't embarrass yourself. Man up. You can handle a cat," Ciaran said and strode away.

Migi rushed over, rubbing against Tadgh's legs and purring. Tadgh rolled his eyes and walked away. Before reaching the car, Tadgh turned around and glared at Migi a couple of times, but she continued to follow him.

"Don't grin at me, cat, I'm not that friendly," Tadgh addressed Migi before he got into the car, knowing full well the gigantic cat would be sitting right next to him.

# CHAPTER 9

It was rare that Ciaran found the air in his master bedroom stuffy. He got off the bed and raised the window slightly. The cold winter breeze rushed into the room. He shut it quickly.

The combination of painkillers and his company's anti-inflammatory medication wasn't pleasant, but it was a lot better than the anesthesia Doctor Thomas had threatened to put him under if he had to perform a surgery to remove the fragment of the bullet Stefan had put in his shoulder the day before.

He turned and looked at Madeline. This beautiful woman had walked into his life in much the same way

Juliette had. Except Madeline had no agenda that he knew of. Would his secrets hurt her? Would she still think of him in the same way if she knew what he had done?

Madeline stirred and opened her beautiful brown eyes. They smiled at him even before she realized he was watching her.

He sat down on the side of the bed. "Go back to sleep," he said and rubbed his thumb over the dimple on her left cheek.

"How's the pain?" she asked groggily.

"Totally gone." He smiled as she rolled her eyes. She pulled him down to kiss him but suddenly stiffened and sat straight up, staring at a corner of the room.

"What is it?" he asked.

"The dots." She jumped off the bed.

"Just ignore them." He tried to pull her back to the bed, but Madeline grabbed her robe and put it on.

"It's the middle of the night," he said, but he could see she wasn't listening to him. Her eyes were fixated on a corner of the room, following what he knew were her psychic blue dots.

"Madeline," he called and grabbed her arm, but she shrugged him off. Ciaran staggered back. She had incredible strength. It didn't even seem like her. Madeline walked along the hall toward the old quarter.

"If you don't talk to me, I won't let you take another step, Madeline." He darted in front of her and blocked her way.

"There are hundreds of blue dots around you, Ciaran. They want me to follow them."

"You've seen them before. Just ignore them."

But instead, she ignored him and kept walking.

"No," he said firmly and held her shoulders. "I want you to go back to the room." Madeline didn't even look like herself anymore. She kept walking, and a moment later, she stood precisely at the place he feared the most—the old lab.

The steel door glared at him in challenge.

"The blue dots showed me the code. If you don't punch it in, I will," she said.

The look in her eyes weakened his knees. Ciaran stared at the door for a long time and then entered a code and the door slid open.

The lights turned on automatically. It was a massive abandoned lab. Vials and jars were scattered on a long, stainless steel workbench. A row of computers sat quietly, gathering dust in a corner of the room. In another corner, there was an enormous steel box that looked like a computer mainframe. Layers of dust coated everything in the room.

He gestured widely at the room. "Well, there it is. The secret place. Are you happy now?" He was nervous, but he didn't know why. A strange, anxious feeling washed over him.

"What are you seeing now, Madeline?"

She smiled. "I saw the blue dots, but they've gone now."

He narrowed his eyes. "So they woke you in the middle of the night, led you here, and then disappeared?"

She shrugged. "Totally random, weren't they?" She glanced around. "What a setup you have here."

He didn't believe her that the dots had gone. He didn't know what game she was playing, but he didn't like it.

"If there's nothing else to see, shall we leave?" he said and headed toward the door.

"What's in the crucifix, and exactly what's in the Golden Life?" she asked.

"They are not related."

"The Golden Life killed Juliette and upset the air bender. He sent Stefan to go after you and the crucifix. As far as I'm concerned, they're related."

The determination in her eyes told him she would find out one way or another. He nodded. "Okay . . . Juliette and I used this lab to create medicine and engineer a lot of unimaginable drugs. Golden Life was a failure, and that's why Juliette died."

"You mentioned you both loved alchemy. Immortality is one of the goals of alchemy, is it not?"

He didn't like where her questions were heading. She couldn't have known this much about the nature of alchemy. "What I wanted wasn't immortality but a medicine that healed all kind of diseases. Reviving a person from death was just the first step."

"So why did you stop?"

"There was one ingredient I didn't approve of—the blood of the living."

Madeline raised an eyebrow. "Have you heard of a blood bank? A lot of people donate blood for medical uses, Ciaran. Why is that such a big deal?"

He shook his head. "Nothing comes cheaply when it comes to saving lives, Madeline. To make a single dose of the medicine to save one life required sacrificial blood from another. That is, the blood had to be drawn from a person until that person died from blood loss. The blood was then distilled into one dose." He was angry now. He could feel his uncontrollable rage coming. He inhaled slowly and lowered his voice. He needed to end the conversation quickly. "Organ donations generally occur *after* the donor dies. With this medicine, even if people consented, removing their blood is an execution. There's no other way to look at it."

He looked at Madeline. "Feel free to judge me, Madeline."

She just looked at him and said nothing.

"I was young and ambitious. I was smart enough to put together an argument that would make the project appear to be morally acceptable. And you know who was my biggest fan and believer?"

She nodded. "Juliette."

"But I couldn't go through with it. I could make the whole world believe in me. I could create a legend. I could change the landscape of science and crap like that. But I wouldn't be able to live with myself. So I pulled the plug on the project."

"It was too late for Juliette?"

He nodded. He raked his hands through his hair. He needed to punch something. "My ambition was contagious. It ate her up like cancer. And you know the rest. So effectually, I killed Juliette."

"No, that's wrong."

"I know what's right and what's wrong, Madeline. I don't care what people think of me or how they judge me. Juliette might have had another agenda when she married me. But she died because of me, and I really don't want the past to be dug up, whatever we might find."

"What about the crucifix?"

"You won't let this go, will you?"

"No."

"If there was a crucifix, and if Juliette did what people claimed she did, she hid some sample gold in the crucifix. Why she chose to use a crucifix rather than other artifacts, I don't know."

"Sample gold?"

"Rumor has it that our family fortune for generations was built on the fact that we have the John Dee's formula to make gold. As far as I know, the rumor is partially incorrect."

"So what's the correct part?"

"Our fortune has something to do with gold, but not until more recently. And we have no ties to John Dee."

"How recent?"

He turned and looked at her. "The attempt to make gold spanned generations of the LeBlancs, but my family was never able to make gold until my time. My father trained me, but I was the one to complete the formula."

"So you can make gold?"

He shrugged. "It was a part of the process I stumbled across in trying to make the Golden Life. It didn't mean much to me, but apparently being able to make gold means a lot to many greedy people. So if the rumor was ever confirmed to be correct, those people would crush our family to dust to get the formula."

"I can imagine."

"We don't exactly make pure gold. Rather, it's a replica of a material that has the same if not better properties. At the end of the day, the gold you dig up from the ground and the gold we make is just a material, a thing. It's valuable because of its properties."

"If Juliette got a sample of your gold and gave it to someone, could they replicate it?"

Ciaran chuckled. "I wouldn't think so. It's not just a formula. It's an alchemical practice."

"Could Juliette do it if she had the formula?"

He nodded. "Maybe. But we'll never know, will we? That's why the air bender was upset when she died. Because even if they had the formula, without her, they couldn't do anything with it."

"So why is Stefan so insistent about finding the crucifix?"

Ciaran shook his head. "I have no idea. Maybe he has no idea that the formula is worthless without the right person to aid in the process. I don't think Stefan exists at the upper end of the food chain. But whoever is paying him might know how to use the formula. Regardless, I don't intend to investigate. We can't change what happened."

Madeline smiled. Strangely, he didn't think she was smiling at him. It wasn't a smile, but more like a look of smugness.

"Do you hear that?" she asked, seeming to look straight through him.

"Hear what?" he asked and turned around to look. No one stood behind him.

"So he said your death was accidental. He cares for you. Whatever your game is, take it elsewhere. Call off your minions." Madeline was talking to the air.

"You can't be talking to Juliette, Madeline. She's dead. Whatever is claiming to be Juliette and talking to you now, it's lying."

"Get the hell out of his life! Out of his home!" Madeline raised her voice.

"This is ludicrous, Madeline. Talk to me!" He tried to get her attention without success. Madeline paced back and forth in the room. He tried to drag her out, but she shoved him away. It was so sudden he wasn't prepared. He staggered back, off balance.

He approached her again but the air grew thicker and seemed to hold him at a distance.

"Air bending. Who are you? Show yourself. Show yourself to me, coward!" Ciaran snarled. "You picked on Madeline because she doesn't know. If you claim to be Juliette, show yourself to me. If you can't, then you are a liar." Nothing happened. "You see, Madeline.

Whoever you are talking to is lying." He tried to get to her, but he couldn't even move an inch toward her.

Madeline still paced and ranted. He could hear part of what she was saying but not all.

"Madeline!" he called out.

Madeline waved her arms in the air. "You want to negotiate? All right!" She darted toward the medicine cabinet. Inside, there was a row of vials. "Which one?" she asked.

"No!" Ciaran yelled at her, but she didn't seem to hear him.

She grabbed one of the tubes and smashed it on the floor. A stream of smoke rose up from the substance and flooded the room.

And that was all he could remember.

## CHAPTER 10

Madeline flopped onto a cold stone floor so hard the she could hear her bones rattle. She couldn't remember much except for some flashes of light and feeling as if she was flying through a tunnel of bright light. Then she awoke here, in a stone chapel.

She glanced around. This wasn't the lab, and Ciaran was nowhere to be seen. She wasn't sure she was even in the same century. She was conscious, and she didn't need to pinch herself to know that. The bone-crushing fall pained her, and it wasn't the sort of pain she would experience in a dream.

She knew the pain of nightmares. She'd had too many of them to count, and this chapel, the air around her, and the feel of the cold breezes and the vivid stench of rotting flesh was much more real than what she would experience in nightmares.

She walked along the dark hall of the chapel, approaching the altar at the far end. Or maybe it was a stone bench rather than an altar. When Madeline got closer, she could see the shadow of someone praying. Hearing Madeline's footsteps, the person turned around. At the same time, large candles on the stone base and torches on the wall lit up.

The woman was stunning. Her long, flaming red hair hung down to her waist. Her milky skin glowed in the flickering light. Her almond-shaped blue eyes gazed at Madeline.

Madeline's instincts told her this was Juliette. A primal corner of her mind whispered to her that this was the woman with whom she was in competition, the woman who held a permanent place in Ciaran's heart.

"Hello, sister," the woman said.

"Hello back."

The woman stepped closer to Madeline, sweeping her long dress across the floor. "I'm Juliette."

She smiled. "I knew that."

"You're smart. Ciaran is always attracted to smart women."

"You studied him thoroughly before you met and married him."

Juliette smiled. "Do you mean I married him with an agenda, as everyone else says?"

"It was a statement, not a question. You don't have to confirm or deny. Ciaran wouldn't care for that. You called, and I responded. Let's talk this out."

"You can see me. That means you have a talent."

"You heard Ciaran. He didn't mean you any harm. Why didn't you leave him alone?"

"Well, I didn't do anything to him, did I? He doesn't have your talent. He can't see me. What can I possibly have done to him?"

"Your brother, Stefan, claimed you sent him a crucifix with Ciaran's family secrets in it. Is that true?"

Juliette smiled. "You're very direct, Madeline."

"It comes with the job."

"Do you love Ciaran?"

"Look, if you are who you say you are, I need answers. Your brother took my best friend, Jo, and if we can't figure out the location of the crucifix, he's going to kill more people, including my friend."

"I no longer have a connection with Stefan. But yes, I did hide away a crucifix for my long-lost family."

"Where?"

"Why do you expect to get things the easy way? The short time I spent with Ciaran, I barely had any of his love. It was all about work. I worked hard, and I devoted myself to him and to his work. I dealt with his mother's harsh judgment and lived in hell for six long months. And I got nothing from it. Why would I want to tell you anything?"

"This isn't a competition, Juliette. Look at you. You're stunning. You're smart. You went to Oxford. I'm a nobody, a reporter from New York. I have no qualifications of the LeBlanc's caliber. Ciaran loved you. He told me so. Your death scarred him for life. Look, all I need is the location of the crucifix so I can rescue my friend from your brother. Then we can go back to New York, and Ciaran will be yours forever."

"Sister! Oh, sister! Talk is so cheap." Juliette walked around, pacing back and forth like an angry cat. "It was his fault for not believing in me. He never believed I loved him."

"Did you? You didn't dig for his family secrets? You didn't scam your way in?"

Juliette looked at Madeline with tears in her eyes. "Yes, I did. I did scam my way in. I was nineteen, and I was raised to do just that, to get inside the LeBlancs. What did you expect me to do?"

"I can't say. I can't speak for you. But just this once, if you've ever loved Ciaran, tell me where the crucifix is."

Juliette laughed bitterly. "And what do I get for telling you?"

"What do you want?" Madeline asked.

"Be careful what you ask for."

"I'll keep my promises. Whatever you think is fair."

Juliette laughed again. "I lived for fairness and believed in good karma. And that is why I ended up dead. What do you think, sister?" Juliette gestured widely at the unflattering chapel in which she resided.

"Just tell me what you want, and I'll see if I can help."

Juliette looked Madeline up and down, and she put on a gracious smile. "If you want to know where the crucifix is, come here. I'll show you." She waved her arm and a ring of fire burst up from the floor, surrounding her. She looked at Madeline and smiled. "I don't have to tell you that the fire is quite hot, do I?"

*This can't be real,* Madeline thought. She stepped toward the fire. Juliette was right. The fire released a terrifying heat.

"This is not a fair fight," she said.

Juliette laughed. "No, it's not. You can have the weapon of your choice. What would you like?"

"A sword." She didn't have to think hard about that one. Fencing was her favourite sport, and she did quite well at it, depending on the type of sword. She'd fare a lot better with a sword in her hand than clawing at Juliette through the fire.

Juliette flicked her finger and a sword dropped down at Madeline's feet. *Where the hell am I? This has to be a dream.* Surely she couldn't die in a dream.

She picked the sword up. It was perfect as if tailored for her.

Madeline looked at Juliette who still stood smiling from the other side of the firewall. Madeline approached the fire and walked through it. The flames were thick and hot. The pain was excruciating. She didn't understand how a dream could hurt so much. Her clothes, her flesh, her bones were burning. A fireball exploded on her chest. She could feel her heart searing.

Madeline couldn't comprehend the pain and didn't think she could make it to the other side, she didn't believe she could survive this fire. If she died in a dream, would she remain in oblivion forever?

Amazed that she was past the fire, she raised the sword and charged at Juliette. Juliette raised her arm, and a sword appeared in her hand. She blocked Madeline's blow. The force of the swords' clash was like an explosion, sending numbing pain straight to Madeline's brain. She was sure it had the same effect on Juliette, as she staggered back and look stunned. Like an angry wolf, Juliette charged at her. She dodged, slashed, swiped, and was surprised that her fighting skills weren't rusty in the least.

Juliette's had what looked like supernatural power. It was not a fair fight. Madeline traded a blow for a blow, a kick for a kick, and a slash for a slash. Juliette raised her sword and charged straight at her without guarding. She was fighting to the death.

Madeline did the same. Her sword stabbed into Juliette's chest, and Juliette's sword did the same to her. The pain was excruciating. The difference between the two of them was that Juliette screamed, and she didn't.

As far as she was concerned, she had won the contest.

Juliette pulled her sword back and waved her arm. Both the fire and the swords vanished. Madeline looked down to see that the wounds on her body had disappeared. But the pain still lingered.

"We're such fools, sister. After all I have done for Ciaran, he has never said he loved me. He has never said the word. He burned my heart. And now he'll burn yours."

"Do you want his love, or do you want him merely to say it? I know men who would say without hesitation that they'd die for their women. But do you think any of them would actually do what they say? None that I know of."

Juliette sneered.

Madeline continued. "As for Ciaran, when he says something to me, I know he means it. He said he loved you, and he said I mattered to him. So how are we stacking up on this love ladder?"

"He was my first, and my last. Why does it matter now?" Juliette laughed until her eyes watered. Then she waved her arm absently. "The crucifix was at Fountains Abbey . . ." Juliette's image flickered, and her expression changed. There were intense emotions in her eyes, very different from what had been there before. "Do not let him find the crucifix. It's not meant for him," Juliette said. Her image flickered again and again. Then her expression returned to what it was before, staged.

Madeline frowned at the inconsistencies in Juliette's statements and expressions. What was going on? "If the crucifix is not meant for Ciaran, who is it for?"

Juliette stared at her blankly. "When did I say it wasn't for Ciaran?"

*You just did. What's with the inconsistency?* "Oh, I had thought you might want to give the crucifix to your brother. Why would Ciaran want it? If I just tell Stefan where it is, would he leave all of us alone?"

Juliette frowned. "Stefan! Yes. My poor brother. He knows nothing. Father wasn't nice to him."

"Where's your father now?"

Juliette looked as if she was daydreaming, and her image flickered so much it almost dissolved. Madeline had a feeling she was talking to two different versions of Juliette, and the flickering one before her was the real one. "Tell me why Ciaran shouldn't find the crucifix?"

"It will kill him. Please don't let him do it. I love him. I never want to harm him."

The image flickered again and again, and then the cold, emotionless Juliette returned. She wiped at a tear running down her face and observed the teardrop on her fingertip. Then she glanced up at Madeline.

"What did you just say?" Juliette asked.

"Nothing. Is this a dream? Am I conscious?" She couldn't think of any other questions to defuse this Juliette's suspicion.

"You're not dreaming. This is my world. It's more real than anything you can ever imagine. This is a hologame."

"A what?"

"A world where I can kill without consequences." Juliette swung her arm, and a dagger appeared out of nowhere. Madeline didn't have time to react before the dagger stabbed her heart.

A hologame? She wasn't sure what that meant, but the blood gushing from her body was definitely real. It wasn't nearly as painful as before. But she could feel her life drifting away. She slumped to the floor.

If this was the last time she would be able think as a human, she might be tempted to use her remaining drop of consciousness to think of Ciaran. But she refused to give up that easily. "For the rest of his life, Ciaran will feel responsible for your death. But that means you're dead to him. Killing me isn't going to help you. And I am not going to die here in your stupid hologame."

Juliette touched Madeline's cheek. Her hands felt cool but very real. "You're a fighter. And I have underestimated you. I haven't set the rules for the game, so I can't kill you now. I'll see you next time, when I set up the game properly and kill you both."

"Whatever you do, you're dead to Ciaran."

"If Ciaran thinks I'm dead, he's mistaken." Her image flickered again and then disappeared into the darkness.

## CHAPTER 11

"Are you sure, Lindsay?"

"Very. I'll get the file delivered to you right after Stefan finishes with it."

"Thank you. I will be at Mon Ciel this morning."

Ciaran put the phone away. Stefan was searching for old records of Juliette's addresses before they were married. *What an idiot!* He should have known Ciaran had tagged all information channels of anything related to Juliette. As soon as Stefan triggered a search, his people would be alerted.

He gazed out at the endless lawn of the manicured back garden, squinting at the sunshine on the beheaded statue of the Goddess of Kindness, the missing head a product of his youth. His father had placed the statue in the garden to remind him of his careless action.

But he was four when it had happened. What would a child of that age know about violence and justice? As far as his four-year-old mind had been concerned, a pack of wild dogs had attacked and killed Dew, his German shepherd, and in retaliation—to blow that pack into pieces—he had mixed the explosive and tested it on the statue. His father had grounded him for a week because of that, and the wild dogs had migrated away from the hillside—a peaceful escape for them, a week of nonviolent activities for him, and injustice for Dew.

It had taken him years to regain the balance of his life after Juliette's death and to find a person who understood him. It had been a lifetime since he was able to fill the void in his soul. And the woman who now completed him was lying on the bed while he stood helpless.

Ciaran glanced back at the bed and saw bead of sweat run down Madeline's forehead. He scrambled back to the bed and wiped the sweat away, and her body began shaking violently as if she was fighting in her dream. He gathered her into his arms and rocked her. If he could take her pain away or fight for her, he would do it.

The compound had exploded in the lab. He didn't know how long it had taken the others to find them lying on the dusty floor. The anesthesia in the compound hadn't agreed with him, and it had taken him hours to regain his consciousness. By the time he awakened, Doctor Thomas was there, telling him there was nothing he could do to wake Madeline.

Her eyes fluttered and opened. She was back. He needed to control his temper and keep his sanity in check. He rubbed his thumb at the dimple on her left cheek and spoke as gently as he could. "Hello there!"

She smiled. "How long have I been out?"

"All night." Ciaran smiled.

"And you didn't sleep?"

"I didn't know when you'd wake." He rubbed at the stubble on his unshaven face and tucked his loose hair back behind his ear. "How are you feeling?"

"I scared you, didn't I?"

"You had a fever. That was all. But you're okay now." He checked the temperature on her forehead with the back of his hand.

"I'm sorry," she said.

"What for?"

"I shouldn't have insisted on seeing the lab and shouldn't have smashed that tube."

He gazed into her eyes and saw a sea of secrets. She was withholding information from him. "Exactly what did you dream about, Madeline?"

She grinned. "I saw us having wild sex in the middle of a jungle, and we somehow ended up on a mountain with lots of naked women running around, and you were the only man there. Then we flew like birds and landed on a tropical beach in Asia. I was drinking fresh coconut juice and you were wearing a Hawaiian shirt."

He brushed a strand of hair from her cheek. "I don't wear Hawaiian shirts."

Madeline laughed. "I feel really good right now and could do with some breakfast. What do you have?"

"I can make you an omelette."

"Sounds wonderful. I'm starving!"

He smiled and nodded. Both he *and* Madeline were lying. He knew it, but he needed a bit more time to get over this hurdle. *What did Juliette want?* He wasn't really sure when she had been alive, and he certainly didn't know now that she was dead.

While Madeline was in the bathroom, he entered a code into a small cabinet in his closet. A small door slid open. He pulled out a watch and snapped a small disk onto its back before putting it on.

This device wasn't finished and hadn't been tested. But if the air bender was the one who had broken into

Mon Ciel and caused all the problems, it would be no different from the pack of wolves that had killed his Dew. The big difference was that his father was no longer around to prevent Ciaran from doing what he considered fair and justified. He intended to give a tit for a tat. And if that took violence, so be it.

Suddenly the air thickened as it had in the museum.

"Air bender," he growled. "The only part of Mon Ciel you get a channel into is my old bedroom. Is this the most you can do here?"

The thick air wrapped around him, but it couldn't create any pressure. Ciaran smiled.

"You believe you opened a hole in Mon Ciel's security. In your dreams! Why don't you show yourself, and then we can talk. Or are you too weak?"

The thick air closed in and tightened around him.

"All right, let's end this."

He raised his watch and turned a small handle. A fan of electric blue light shone out, cutting through the thick air and lighting the entire room. When the light lit up the far wall, instead of seeing the old man as he had expected, he saw the shape of a woman.

Juliette.

Ciaran jerked his arm back, and the electric light swung in the air, hit the ceiling, and bounced back to him. He was thrown against the cabinet door, collapsing a shelf.

He must have hit his head because he saw stars. His vision was blurry. He heard Juliette's voice, "Try the Primer. I want to talk to you. I miss you, Ciaran."

He shook his head. "You're dead, Juliette."

"I want to see you again, Ciaran. Take the Primer . . ."

The voice echoed away and vanished. He knew he'd been lucky. If the device had been perfected, he could have electrocuted himself. He must have a concussion as it was. But it was better than being dead.

Madeline rushed into the closet. "What happened? Are you okay?"

"Just a stupid accident." He sat up and wrapped his arm around her shoulders so that she could haul him up from the floor.

Madeline glanced around. "You accidentally flew into the cabinet?"

Ciaran shook his head. "I've got some information about Stefan's whereabouts. We might be able to track him precisely in a few hours."

"That's great news. Can you walk? Should I call Doctor Thomas?"

"I'm okay." He glanced at the corner of the room where he had seen the shape of Juliette and saw nothing. Then he caught the faint scent of vanilla and roses in the air.

"Do you smell that?" he asked.

"Yes. It wasn't here before. What just happened, Ciaran?"

He shook his head. "I don't know."

"Oh, no." Madeline held her ears and winced. "It's Juliette's voice. She's in the old lab."

# CHAPTER 12

In the hallway in the new quarter, Tadgh was negotiating with Migi. "Okay, listen sweetheart, I'm about to go into the men's room. And you are *not* following me there!"

The cat waved her twin tails patiently in different directions, then sat down and thumped them on the floor.

"Come on. Be patient. When Doctor Thomas brings TJ back from the vet, you can be friends with him and leave me alone. He's only a puppy, but he's a lot of fun."

Thump. Thump.

"Cats don't thump their tails. And could you try to be a bit more ladylike?"

Thump. Thump. Thump.

"All right, I'll ignore you then."

Before Tadgh could leave for the bathroom with the intention of sneaking out the other side and going straight to the kitchen for a quick breakfast, Migi jumped up. Her hair stood on end, and her tails pointed straight to the ceiling, the tips waving rapidly. The cat hissed and meowed and slapped the air with her paws, talons unsheathed.

"Come on. Don't act like that or people will think I hit you."

The cat continued to hiss.

"We might disagree on things, but this is completely unnecessary. What do you want?"

Tadgh felt a chill run up his spine. He turned around and saw only the empty hallway. But someone was calling his name. He couldn't see anyone.

He felt an urge to do something, go somewhere. Tadgh glanced around again.

The hallway lit up toward the old quarter of the house. He followed the light. Part of him didn't want to, but it seemed natural to go.

Migi clawed at his jeans and meowed loudly.

*Why is she doing that?* Tadgh shook his head and kept walking.

In no time, he stood in front of the old lab. His mind went blank, and he had no idea what the code was to get in. He had never entered the lab by himself. Ever.

Suddenly, the security pad lit up by itself. The code was right there, highlighted for him. In the back of his mind, something was screaming for him to stop.

It had to be the cat. Tadgh sneered and pushed the door open. He walked along the shelves, tracing his finger over rows and rows of jars full of chemicals. Ciaran's stuff. Tadgh shook his head.

"How on Earth could anyone find chemicals and potions interesting?" Tadgh muttered to himself. Ciaran was only two years older than he, but his big brother was way too complicated for him to even think about understanding.

Tadgh chuckled. He swayed a bit and felt drunk.

What was he doing in this old lab? His family owned a pharmaceutical company, but when it came to medicine, the most he ever had to deal with was taking a few aspirin when he had a headache.

A jar full of some kind of chemical in front of him caught his eye. He reached his hand out to grab it, ignoring the screaming voice in his head telling him not to.

The cat flew at him and bit his hand. Tadgh dropped the jar, but it didn't break.

"Ouch! You stupid cat." He bent to pick up the jar.

Migi darted at him with the force of a leopard and knocked Tadgh on his backside. "Okay, that's enough, cat. I'll kick you if you come near me again. I really will. Don't tempt me!"

Tadgh grabbed the jar, and the cat slapped at it with her paw, making it fall to the floor again.

"You're pissing me off, Migi!" He scrambled to grab the jar again.

"Come near me, and I'll smash this over your head."

Migi withdrew, hissing from a distance.

Ciaran and Madeline rushed to the door of the lab and stood there, breathing heavily.

"What are you two doing here?" Tadgh grinned.

"Put that jar down," Ciaran said.

"Why?" Tadgh said and pulled the lid off. "I'm making something here. I have a headache." Ciaran gestured for Madeline to stay outside the lab and approached his brother.

"Want to help me?" Tadgh waved the jar.

"Sure," Ciaran said, reaching his hand out. "But give me the jar." Ciaran took the jar from Tadgh and put the lid back on.

Tadgh's vision started to blur. His head wasn't functioning properly. It must be the headache. "Aren't you going to whip something up for me?" Tadgh shook his head, trying to stay alert.

"I will," Ciaran said. "Why don't you go back to your room to rest? I'll bring you some medicine."

Tadgh nodded. He took a couple of steps then turned back to Ciaran. "Hey, you tricked me. You just don't want me to touch your stuff!"

"It's not my stuff, it's Juliette's. You need something for your headache — I'll take care of it. Get out of here, Tadgh."

"Oh, no, no, you don't understand." Tadgh came back in and pointed to the cabinet at the far corner. "The jar you're holding and *this* jar will make a dream potion." Tadgh pulled the cabinet door open.

"No, Tadgh. Don't touch anything in there!" Ciaran approached.

"It's not poison or anything." Tadgh picked up a bottle. "This stuff and that jar will make a primer."

"A what?"

"The Dream Primer. Here, I'll show you."

"No, no. Give me the bottle. I'll do it for you. I promised."

His brother had promised. Ciaran always kept his promises. "All right," he said. But just as he was about to give it to Ciaran, someone was screaming at him in his head, telling him Ciaran was lying. The voice told him to take the bottle and run.

So he ran.

Ciaran grabbed him from behind. "Leave the bottle."

"No."

A scuffled commenced, and the bottle slipped out of his hand. Ciaran grabbed it before it could hit the floor.

"Tadgh, get out of here!" Ciaran shoved him, pushing him out of the lab.

Tadgh shoved back. "Don't you push me around, big brother."

"Out! Out!" Ciaran kept pushing to no avail, so he landed a punch on Tadgh's face.

Tadgh saw stars. But he didn't give in. He charged at Ciaran. Ciaran put the bottle on the lab bench, grabbed his arms, and kicked his legs out from under him.

Tadgh crashed to the floor.

Madeline flew into the lab and sat on him, pinning his arms to the floor, while Ciaran rushed to a cabinet, coming back with a needle.

The two of them were ganging up against him. Tadgh kicked hard but couldn't get free of Madeline's grip.

Ciaran shoved the needle into Tadgh's neck and pumped the fluid into his vein. Tadgh wriggled and threw Madeline off. He sprung up to his feet and ran. But he only made it a couple of steps before his world went dark.

He screamed and turned around. There, he saw Juliette. "Juliette!" Tadgh cried out.

She reached her arms out to him, but they turned into giant snakes, wrapping around his neck and strangling him.

# CHAPTER 13

Tadgh yelled out Juliette's name and sat up on his bed abruptly, panting. Madeline rushed to the bed and grabbed his hands, pulling them away from his neck as he gasped for air. She understood very well how disoriented he must feel coming out of unconsciousness.

He looked at Madeline then glanced around his bedroom. Madeline pulled him in to her arms for an embrace. She held him until the vibration of emotion in his body settled. "You're okay now. Ciaran has just gone to talk to Doctor Thomas. He'll be back soon."

Tadgh eased out of Madeline's hug.

"What happened?" he asked.

"You went into the old lab, apparently trying to mix something up. Ciaran had to knock you out before you intoxicated yourself."

Tadgh rubbed at his forehead, trying to recall. He shook his head and flopped back to the bed on his back. "I can't remember any of it."

"It'll take time. But it will come back to you."

"Can I have some coffee?"

"I'm not sure if that's good for you right now. I'll ask Ciaran."

Tadgh sat up, arching an eyebrow. Madeline laughed. "All right, all right. I'll get you some coffee." She stood to leave the room.

"No need to go to the kitchen, Madeline." Tadgh got off the bed. He held onto the bed post for a short moment to steady himself. Madeline rushed over to help him, but he waved his arm absently. "I've got it. Thanks."

He opened a wall cabinet, revealing a coffeemaker and several containers of biscuits and sweet treats. He turned around and grinned at her.

"Ciaran stocks spirits and wine and you stockpile coffee and sweet treats."

Tadgh laughed. "I don't have gadgets in my room like he does."

Madeline glanced around. Ciaran had a gigantic wall-sized screen in his room, but Tadgh didn't even have a TV. Ciaran had a computer system set up in a corner of his room, so complicated that Madeline didn't even know how to turn it on. But in here, Madeline couldn't even see a remote control.

"I'm not anti-technology, if that's what you're thinking. I travel a lot and just don't generally need gadgets. Coffee?"

Madeline nodded.

Tadgh brought the coffee over to the bed. He climbed onto it and sat cross-legged. He placed a small plate of cookies in the middle of the bed and pushed it toward Madeline.

"How are you feeling, Tadgh?"

"Still a bit queasy. But I'll be fine after this." He raised his mug of coffee.

"What did you see? You can tell me, and then I'll tell you what I saw."

"What you saw last night when you scared the hell out of Ciaran?"

"What?"

"We found you both in the lab, unconscious. When Ciaran was up and Doctor Thomas told him there was nothing he could do to wake you, man, I've never seen him like that before."

"Like what?"

Tadgh shook his head and bit his cookie. "When Juliette died, he was devastated. But it was more like sorrow, or maybe regret. But he seemed to accept her death. But last night, he was furious. He wouldn't consider even the slightest possibility that he might lose you. It was madness."

"He didn't say much this morning."

"I'd be surprised if he had. He's a control freak. I should ask Mother if he even cried as a baby. I doubt it very much."

"Have you heard from Jennifer?"

"Yes. She called. She'd back to Dublin now. Wouldn't talk to Ciaran! You can see where Ciaran got his hard head."

From the door, Migi walked in graciously in and hopped on to the bed. She lay down next to Tadgh and purred loudly.

"You haven't asked for permission to come in, let alone to get in bed with me, lady."

Madeline laughed. Migi moved over to lay next to Madeline. She scratched the cat's ears, making her purr louder. Tadgh shook his head and sipped his coffee.

"Do you like Juliette?"

"What?" Tadgh choked on his coffee.

"You heard me, Tadgh."

Tadgh reached to Migi to scratch her ears, but she inched out of Tadgh's reach. Madeline looked at Tadgh, waiting for an answer.

Tadgh cleared his throat. That was exactly what Ciaran did before he said anything difficult, Madeline thought.

"Ciaran is the smart guy in the family. He was home schooled, but by about fourteen, he had mastered all the subjects—chemistry, medicine, artificial intelligence, computer science, you name it— at a university level. And at sixteen, he ran our business empire. Our family business had grown tenfold since he took it over . . ."

Tadgh leaned back and stretched his legs out. "You might think our parents forced him to study. But that wasn't the case. And look at me! I went to college just to keep up appearances." Tadgh sipped his coffee and looked at Madeline over the rim. "Ciaran has loved to learn ever since he was a kid. He's always been hungry for knowledge. And not just learning and accepting things the way they are. He loves to *create*." Tadgh gazed at Madeline. "You might not like this, Madeline, but in that regard, Ciaran and Juliette were a perfect match."

"And how can you be so sure I don't love knowledge and creation?"

Tadgh shook his head. "Apart from a slight physical resemblance, Ciaran and I have nothing in common. I'm not perfect and never try to be. Ciaran thinks he has to be perfect and has to be responsible for everything."

Madeline nodded and leaned against the bedpost.

"Juliette was a perfect match for Ciaran. She was almost a mirror image of him, just in a different gender."

"And isn't a perfect match a good thing?"

Tadgh shook his head again. "It's like having two right shoes."

Madeline chuckled. "Interesting analogy."

"You haven't been with him for a long time, Madeline. And I don't know you at all. But I'm telling you this even though Ciaran will shoot me if he finds out. When Doctor Thomas said he couldn't wake you, I swear I saw tears in Ciaran's eyes."

Madeline nodded. "I appreciate you telling me."

"It's more for me than for you. It's nice to see my brother has some feelings again," Tadgh muttered. "I knew Juliette was using my brother. But there's nothing I can do about it because she's dead now . . ."

"I don't think so."

"Excuse me?"

Then she explained to him about the blue dots.

"When I was in the coma, I talked to Juliette, and she told me she might not have died."

Tadgh narrowed his eyes. "You dreamed about Juliette, and she said she didn't die?"

"It wasn't just a dream. I intentionally inhaled the drug so that I could talk to her. Don't question it, Tadgh, just accept it. She haunted Ciaran, and I wanted to know what was going on."

Tadgh stared blankly. "I think I need more coffee." He rushed to the cabinet to get some more brewing.

"It wasn't a dream. I fought with Juliette, and there was this." Madeline opened a button on her shirt and pulled the collar aside. On the left side of her chest, there was a nasty red scar from a stab wound.

Tadgh stared, speechless at the sight of the raw wound.

"There were more, but they all vanished except for this one. I was supposed to die from this wound. It wasn't a dream, Tadgh. She said she would come back for Ciaran. The thing is, though, it seemed as if I was talking to two different versions of Juliette. One was cold and calculated, and the other one was sad."

"I bet it was the cold bitch who stabbed you."

"That's not what I'm concerned about. She told me the location of the crucifix."

Tadgh choked badly on his coffee. When he got his breath back, he asked, "Where?"

"It's at Fountains Abbey."

"What?"

"Fountains Abbey."

"Do you know anything about that place?"

"No."

"There are miles and miles of national parks and tourist attractions. You've got to be kidding me!"

"I'm not making it up. And that's not my main concern."

"So what is?"

"After the cold Juliette revealed the location of the crucifix, the sad one told me not to let Ciaran find it, that it wasn't meant for him."

"So who is it for then? Stefan?"

"She said if Ciaran found the crucifix, it would kill him."

"Why? Is there a bomb in it?"

"I don't know. Poison maybe? A toxic chemical? Whatever it is, I'm not telling him until I figure out what she meant."

"Agreed. If he knows, he'll be the first one there. And then we'll need a bulldozer to get him off the issue. That's no good if we need to defuse a bomb at the same time. But how do you plan to find out what's going on? Talk to Juliette?"

"No, I'm not ready to do that again. I'll take a look at the site myself."

"I'll go with you."

"Go where?" Ciaran asked from the doorway.

# CHAPTER 14

Madeline pushed at Ciaran's chest, backing him into his office. The sunlight poured in via a tall window at the far end of the room. The frame of the window and the light haloed behind Ciaran, making him look to her like a doomed angel. The sight of him made her stomach churn.

He smiled at her. "Explain to me why you suddenly want to have a picnic at a national park with Tadgh?"

Needing to distract him from the current issue of the crucifix, she turned on her best weapon, her sultry voice. "And why not?" She wrapped her arms around his neck. "I'll take Migi, TJ, and you as well, if you're interested."

Ciaran's voice was already muffled with the kiss. "It's quite convenient actually. Stefan just called your phone. I picked up, so he was a bit disappointed. He wanted to meet at a national park."

She stopped the kiss. "Which one?"

"The national park next to Rufford Abbey."

She withheld a sigh of relief. If the crucifix was actually at Fountains Abbey, Ciaran wouldn't accidentally stumble upon it at Rufford Abbey. "All right. Is Jo okay?"

"Yes. She sounded fine."

"Stefan let you talk to her?"

"Not voluntarily. But a man has to know how to negotiate, doesn't he? The meeting isn't on for another few hours. So we have time."

"Why didn't you tell me in front of Tadgh?"

"I don't want to have to worry about him."

"He looked all right in the room. You're worried about what happened in the lab?"

Ciaran nodded.

"Wouldn't it be better to have him by your side than leaving him at home?"

Ciaran shook his head. "I'm sending him to our Paris headquarters. It will keep him busy. He gets along well with my cousin, George, there."

"You'll need a bulldozer," Madeline muttered.

"I beg your pardon?"

She smiled and kissed him again until all of the knotted muscles in his body loosened. With just a slight push, he was on the couch with her on top. She tugged at his shirt, pulling it, desperately getting to the flesh and the firmness of his toned muscles.

This man knew how to touch a woman. All of her senses exploded, her body relaxed, and she felt as if she'd melt under his touch and evaporate into thin air. He ravished her mouth then tugged at her shirt and pulled it off.

And that was when he saw it—a big red scar on the left side of her chest.

*Damn!* Madeline cursed to herself. She had totally forgotten about the mark.

"What's this? It wasn't there the night before."

"It's a burn."

"This is a scar, Madeline, not a new wound. How did it happen?"

Madeline pulled her shirt down to cover her exposed breast. "I fought with Juliette during the coma. She stabbed me, and I didn't duck fast enough. I gave her a few good blows, though."

Ciaran sat up on the couch. "Say that again, please!"

"I fought with Juliette. She told me it wasn't a dream. It was a hologame, whatever that means."

Ciaran narrowed his eyes. "She told you that she got you into a hologame?"

"That's what she said. What's a hologame, Ciaran?"

Ciaran smiled and teased Madeline hair. "You've seen a hologram, haven't you?"

She nodded.

"At a very advanced level of technology, instead of using telephone, we use holograms to communicate, and we call it holocast. A holocast can not only send hologram images but can actually teleport a person as well. That is, if the communicators *choose* to step out of a holocast."

Madeline blinked. "Better than *Star Wars!*"

Ciaran chuckled. "A hologame uses the same technology to allow players to compete in a virtual environment. I'm testing the technology at the moment."

"You invented it?"

Ciaran laughed. "I invented my own version of it. But there are others who have their own technology."

"How many others?"

"There are a handful of manufacturers in the world. It's very cost-prohibitive."

Madeline chuckled. "I'm sure it takes more than money."

Ciaran nodded. "But what you experienced—if it truly was a hologame—is unheard of. It was played under subconscious conditions—that's like playing using your mind. Any technology that plays with the mind is dangerous and immoral. Especially, when it's done without your consent."

His eyes darkened now. She recalled Tadgh telling her how helpless Ciaran had felt when she didn't wake. "Juliette had my partial consent. Please don't make her angrier with you."

"What do you mean?"

"Her blue dots and her voice kept accusing you of killing her. I just wanted her to stop haunting you and this house. I agreed to talk to her, and she told me to smash the tube in the lab."

The fury shooting from his eyes was like a laser. Ciaran stood and strode toward the window, staring outside. She knew he was trying to control his temper. She said nothing else.

When he turned around, his eyes were completely dark, and his voice was so low that it sounded like a growl. "Don't you ever put yourself between me and my problem. Juliette is *my* problem. I alone will deal with her, just as I have in the past I don't know how many years."

"Well, you didn't exactly do a good job."

"I'm handling it."

"How? By not talking about it? By stopping everyone in your family from discussing it or helping you?"

"I don't need your help. Or anyone else's."

"I'm sorry I hurt your ego." She put her hands on her hips.

"Ego! You think this has to do with my *ego*?"

"Give me a better explanation then, Ciaran."

"You don't know what Juliette was capable of when she was alive. And she's worse now that she's dead. The people you're talking to are Juliette's allies, and they can crush you before you even know what's happening. You're far too important for me to lose. And if you take that lightly, then *that* hurts my ego!" He hit a vase. It flew to the wall and fell shattered to the floor, along with her nerves. "I'm sorry I've scared you." He flopped down to the couch and put his head in his hands.

She embraced him from behind. "Please tell me you forgive me."

He turned around and pulled her into his arms. "There is nothing to forgive, Madeline. I'm sorry, I didn't mean to yell."

"Say sorry to the vase!"

He smiled, although it didn't quite travel to his eyes. "It would take a load off me if you could refrain yourself from any drastic action toward people you don't know."

She tucked his long hair behind his ears, reached up, and kissed his cheek. "I promise."

Ciaran's phone buzzed. "Lindsay . . . All right. Thanks." He hung up the phone and rushed toward his computer. Madeline followed.

Opening a file, he skimmed through rows and rows of data and codes. Then he turned off the computer and stood up.

"We need to leave now. We are going to Laurent's place and then off to Rufford Abbey."

"What just happened, Ciaran?"

"I'll explain on the way. The data is Stefan's computer search pattern. He just tapped into Laurent's home computer. I want to make sure everything is okay."

"Why Laurent?"

"She was Juliette's best friend."

Before they reached the door, Tadgh approached with a grin on his face. "Going to a picnic without me?"

# CHAPTER 15

An hour later, they arrived at Stow-on-the-Wold. They had been here before for Robert's funeral, the day after the Fosse Way saga. Madeline remembered the lawn, the house, and the sad aura it had had at the time.

She was sure that, as the head of the LeBlancs' security, Robert's death wouldn't have left his own family in limbo. But after what had happened at Mon Ciel, she thought they would be able to leave this behind them. But no, here they were here again, seeing the widow and the child.

But things had indeed changed since the funeral. The sad aura was gone. The widow Laurent greeted them at the front door. Her eyes were warm and contented. Laurent had had to get on with life for her daughter's sake, Madeline thought.

"Oh, Tadgh, you look so well! It's so good to see you."

"You are beautiful, as always. I am desperate to see the baby Bella!"

"She's asleep, but she'll be up soon. Come on in."

When everyone had settled around the coffee table, Laurent asked Ciaran, "Why now, Ciaran? For so many years, you refused to touch any of her belongings. Is it worth it to dig up old memories now?"

"It's a long story. I need to have a look at her journals, or anything about what she did before we got married. Also, I've reserved a very nice holiday home overseas where you can stay. You need a break from all this."

"Are you evacuating us, Ciaran? What's going on?"

"I've lost Robert, and there's nothing I can do to bring him back. But I can't let anything happen to you and Bella. Just go for a short time. It would give me peace of mind. Please."

Laurent sighed. "All right, very well then. The room is intact. Help yourself to anything in it."

"You kept her room all these years?" Ciaran was astonished.

"We were like sisters. You're not the only one who can't let go, Ciaran. She used it occasionally after you got married as well. Whenever she was confused, desperate, lonely, or just needed a shoulder, she'd come here."

"I'm sorry . . ." Ciaran began.

Tadgh cleared his throat. "I think the baby is crying. Could I please see her, Laurent? I'm good with kids. I promise I won't scare her or anything."

Madeline knew there was no baby crying. Tadgh was a master at distraction. As his mother had said, he knew Ciaran's weakness.

Laurent stood and smiled at Ciaran and Madeline. "All right then, you two can head to the room. You know where it is, Ciaran. I'll take Tadgh to see the baby so he'll stop nagging. I have something else for you, too, Ciaran."

They parted ways.

Juliette's room was neat, tidy, and minimal. There was nothing nonessential. No flowers, vases, paintings, or decorative items. A single bed was tucked into a corner, and a desk sat in front of a small window.

On the desk was a small computer, books, journals, and other reading material, all neatly arranged. The room was well-maintained, so much so that Madeline wagered she wouldn't be able to find a single speck of dust in here.

On a small shelf, there were more books and a picture of Ciaran and Juliette that had been taken in front of the Bodleian Library at the University of Oxford. They looked so happy. Ciaran looked exactly the same, his long black hair swept back, almost touching his shoulders.

Ciaran muttered something and was about to remove the picture from the shelf, but Madeline stepped in and grabbed it before he could. "Look at you! You wore your hair long, even back then." Ciaran just smiled and continued to scour the room for notebooks and journals.

Madeline found a large wooden box and opened it. Inside, there she found tiny jars and tubes containing eye shadows, lipsticks, and lip balms. It looked like Juliette was trying to create her own line of makeup. There was also a small bottle of perfume. Madeline thought Juliette had probably made that, as well.

The box looked as if it had another layer. She dug her fingernails in and tried to lift the surface shelf. The velvet-covered bottom popped up. "What do we have here?"

Ciaran turned around and came closer to take a look. Peeling the fake bottom off, they found a smaller box with a rusty lid underneath. Ciaran rubbed the rust off to see what was written there. It read "Dream Primer."

Ciaran put the box down on the bed quickly and pulled Madeline away from it. "It's a primer. She had been making this all along. What's it for?" Ciaran asked, mostly to himself.

Ciaran grabbed a large folder from the shelf. Inside, there were several articles, pictures, and notes. He picked up an article. The title read, "Susceptibility to Hypnosis." He picked up another one. "Neurological Fantasy." Ciaran shook his head and muttered, "I didn't know she was into these subjects."

Then he picked up a note with her handwritten text and a diagram. The diagram looked like a flow chart and had many wavy lines coming in and out of boxes and bubbles. "Electrical waves . . . Brain waves . . ." Ciaran talked to himself. He turned the note aside to read the tiny print. "Dreamer Primer," Ciaran read out loud.

They heard a loud bang and saw a fireball hit the glass window. The glass shattered. The curtain and the rod collapsed on Ciaran and Madeline. Ciaran dropped everything he was holding, pulling Madeline aside.

They both dropped to the floor as another fireball flew in and hit the bed. The linens caught on fire and spread with lightning speed. Ciaran grabbed Madeline and pulled her with him out of the room.

They heard Tadgh shouting to get out from the other end of the house. At the end of the hallway, they could see him helping Laurent, who was carrying the baby.

It looked as if the back room of the house and the kitchen was on fire. They could hear the footsteps of people running outside and some on the roof. They met in the living room.

Both Ciaran and Tadgh pulled out their guns and pushed the women protectively behind them. Ciaran looked toward the kitchen and saw a spark. They kicked the door open and stormed outside. The gas tank in the kitchen exploded behind them, and the house burst into flames.

"Get in the car," Ciaran said. As they ran toward the car, a fireball dropped and exploded in front of it, stopping them from getting inside.

They withdrew from the vehicle.

Three men in black, all wearing masks, ran after them from the back of the house.

The house was quite remote and did not have any next-door neighbors. But it did sit close to the road. A car passing by approached and stopped when the driver saw the house on fire. A couple got out. Two men in masks rushed out from the side of the house to shoot at them. A series of small darts flew out and hit the car's passengers.

Ciaran, Madeline, and Tadgh had seen this weapon before at Mrs. Hanson's place. The tourists evaporated into thin air, leaving only piles of empty clothes behind.

Ciaran shot at a man approaching them. Tadgh took another one down.

The third one pointed his gun right at Madeline. But when he saw her face clearly, he didn't shoot. Taking the opportunity, Ciaran put a bullet in the man's head.

The baby cried in Laurent's arms.

The two who had just shot the couple took shelter behind a tree so that Ciaran and Tadgh couldn't get a good shot. Despite Ciaran yelling at her, Madeline ran out and grabbed two wood panels standing against the garden fences.

They could use these as shields against the darts, Madeline thought. Whoever those people were, they apparently wouldn't shoot her.

Ciaran cursed and grabbed the panels, pushing Madeline behind him. Tadgh grabbed the other panel, and blocked Laurent and the baby.

Five men appeared from the left and five from the right. They charged forward, kicking at the panels. But they didn't shoot.

Ciaran took down two more, and Tadgh fired at one of them.

There were more men coming. The masked men kept charging at the panels until one of them got past. He grabbed Ciaran and kneed him in his cracked rib. Ciaran slumped to the ground, heaving in pain.

Tadgh turned around and received a kick that sent him to the ground as well.

The five men in masks charged toward the women and children.

Madeline picked up a steel bar lying nearby and whacked at the coming men without mercy. She sent three of them to the ground, perhaps with cracked skulls.

The other two were grabbed from behind by Ciaran and Tadgh. While the men fought, Madeline guided Laurent, still carrying the baby, to the car.

They traveled only a short distance before five more men charged over from the other side of the road. These five had the dart guns in their hands.

Ciaran could see it was too far to reach the women before they were shot. One man gave Madeline a kick, sending her skidding away on the ground.

Ciaran and Tadgh pulled their guns and fired at the five men. Four went down, and the last one shot at Laurent and the baby before was killed by Ciaran.

Ciaran and Tadgh hurried over, and Ciaran helped Madeline up. "Were you shot?" he asked.

"No, I'm fine," she said.

Then Ciaran ran over to Laurent and the baby.

"No, no, no, please no!" Ciaran looked helplessly at the two of them, who were fast fading away. Soon, like the others, mother and daughter became just piles of clothes.

Lying next to Laurent's clothes was a book, Juliette's diary. Laurent had kept the diary in her own room and wanted to give it to Ciaran. Luckily, it had not been destroyed in the fire.

Madeline grabbed Ciaran and hugged him tightly while his body shook in uncontrollable grief.

Tadgh kicked the fence furiously. "Who the fuck were those people? What the fuck do they want?"

There was nothing more here for them to see or do. There was nothing left except for piles of clothes where people used to exist. Ciaran stood up, grabbed the diary, and moved numbly toward his car. His face was cold, his eyes burned with anger.

Five more men appeared across the road.

"You've got to be fucking kidding me," Tadgh said.

Ciaran said nothing. He pulled out his gun and shot three men down at once. The other two charged forward with lightning speed, leaping onto Ciaran's car, one of them giving Ciaran a flying kick on his way down. Ciaran slid away on the ground. The diary dropped out of his hand. The other man attacked Tadgh.

The one who had just kicked Ciaran walked toward the diary to pick it up. Before he could reach it, he copped a metal bar in the head from Madeline.

He was down and stayed down.

The last man had been incapacitated by Tadgh.

Ciaran picked up the diary, put it in his jacket pocket, and walked to the car. Madeline and Tadgh followed.

# CHAPTER 16

Ciaran got behind the wheel. Madeline was in the front seat, and Tadgh was in the back.

Ciaran had just started the car up when they heard the roar of an engine and saw a car hurtling toward them. Ciaran gave a half smile and geared up his car.

Tadgh was silent. He braced himself and did his best to hold his organs in place.

Ciaran's car zoomed out to the road, fishtailed at the corner of the driveway, and left behind nothing but smoke for the other car.

Madeline looked in the rear view mirror and saw Tadgh was sweating as if just out of a shower. His eyes were shut tight. Ciaran smiled. "Speed is Tadgh's worst nightmare."

The chasing car didn't give up easily. Ciaran drove to a back road and continued in a direction which led away from Rufford Abbey.

The back country roads were not kind to Tadgh as Ciaran drove with highway speed on rural, two-way country roads meant to hold only one car at a time. Madeline thought she had a strong stomach, but sometimes she felt her organs might just erupt through her ribcage.

Ciaran kept his eyes fixed straight ahead, shifting gears and turning corners as if he was driving in a grand prix. His face was cold as steel. Sometimes, inches from hitting stone fences or trees, Madeline gasped. But Ciaran didn't even blink.

Ciaran knew these roads well. At an approaching sharp corner, he hit the brake, veered to the other side of the road, and smoothly turned. The other car went straight through the corner and into a fast flowing creek.

"Farewell," Ciaran said dryly and drove back in the direction of Rufford Abbey.

Shortly afterward, Madeline, Ciaran, and Tadgh approached a small rest stop in the middle of deer hunting ground. They found Stefan and Jo waiting.

As they entered, Madeline could see that Tadgh was dazzled by Jo. She was a petite girl, barely reaching his shoulder. Her long, black hair framed a foxy face, mysteriously brightened by her large green eyes.

Jo's eyes widened when she saw Ciaran. "White Knight," she said.

"Hello, Jo. It's a pleasure to meet you face to face." Ciaran nodded in greeting.

Madeline smiled at Jo in reassurance. They didn't need to talk to communicate.

"I'm Tadgh, Ciaran's brother." Tadgh approached to shake hands with Jo, but Stefan waved his finger to stop his motion.

"This is not a party."

Jo gave Tadgh a bright smile that weakened his knees.

"Very nice to meet you, Tadgh. I can tell you're Ciaran's brother. Do you play hologames?"

"I said, this is not a party," Stefan cut in.

Jo winked at Tadgh. "We'll play later."

Ciaran couldn't hide a smile. "All right, we're here. Now tell us what you want, Stefan."

Let the opponent draw blood first, Madeline thought. That was the Ciaran approach she admired.

"Jo can only decode half the disk. I want you to do the other half for me. Otherwise . . ." Stefan turned

Jo's shoulder slightly so that everyone could see the gun he had pointed at her back. "Let's move it up a bit." He shifted the gun up, pointing it at the back of Jo's head. "And now let's get cozy." He pulled Jo with his left hand, pressing her body against his and wrapping his left arm around her. He pointed the gun at her temple. "One wrong move, and I'll blow her head off."

Jo smiled. "He's been saying that for two days."

Stefan pressed the gun harder against her head.

"Hey, hey, hang on," Tadgh interrupted. "You want us to do something, right? I don't know shit about computers. Which half did Jo translate or decode or whatever you call it? Was it the first half or the second half, or did she translate every second word?"

Stefan's face reddened. "You think this is a joke?"

Madeline swallowed her laugh.

"It's the last one . . . unfortunately," Jo spoke gently.

"What the fuck do you mean by that? You told me you've got fifty percent done," Stefan fumed.

"I did, but I did bits and pieces," Jo explained.

"Program coding is complicated, Stefan. I'm sure Juliette told you that. There will be a part that Jo has enough experience to decode. But there will be part that only I can decode because I have the experience in that area. It's not necessarily about who has better skills. It's the experience that makes the difference." Ciaran smiled at Jo.

"I don't give a shit. I don't care how you do it. I want the information in one piece — and in English."

"Stefan, Ciaran and Jo have to work together to decode the document for you. I'm sure you understand that," Madeline added.

"Then you'll all have to come with me," Stefan said.

"We need *real* computers to do it. Remember, Stefan, Juliette used my computer to code this disk. Our technology is the most sophisticated in this country. So can you arrange that?"

"He has a piece of junk in his room he calls a computer," Jo teased.

"You think I'm stupid? You think I'm just going to give you the disk and let you go? Or follow you back to your place so that you can pull a gun on me?"

Ciaran responded. "I'm not suggesting any such thing. And besides, you're the one pulling guns here. The crucifix isn't even what you really want. You want the gold — and you think my family can make gold, maybe out of thin air. You believe that Juliette got some gold somehow — or the know-how from our family — and sent it to you in the crucifix. The truth is, we don't make gold, and no such method to do it exists. Look, why don't we just give you some money . . ."

Tadgh interrupted, "No shit. I'm not giving him any money. You can hang on to the disk and half of the information, if you want. I could care less. But that very beautiful person standing next to you is a good friend of Madeline, and Madeline is almost my sister-in-law . . ."

"What?" Jo and Madeline said at the same time.

Ciaran looked at Tadgh. "Now you *are* talking shit."

"You married her because you had sex with her," Tadgh sneered.

"You don't think I'd marry just anyone I've had sex with, do you?" Ciaran scolded.

"Come on, bro. You get too serious about casual sex."

"Casual sex?" Ciaran raised his voice.

"Sorry, it was me. I'm the one-night-stander. But I've already given Juliette some money. She was smoking hot. I've already spent a lot of money on her. So no more money for him." Tadgh pointed at Stefan.

"What the fuck do you mean by that?" Ciaran snarled.

"It was before you got married. Come on! A pretty girl like Juliette? You were out and about with your big deal business. You thought she'd sit around and wait for you?"

"Tadgh!"

"Oh, don't tell me you thought she was a virgin, bro. She . . ."

Stefan screamed, "Shut up, shut up! Don't you two fuck around with me!"

He was so angry he swung the gun, pointing it at Tadgh, and thus took it away from Jo's head. At the same time, Ciaran and Tadgh pulled their guns and pointed them at Stefan.

"Don't move," Ciaran said.

"Two of us and one of you—better keep the gun there. Don't move an inch, you stupid son-of-a-bitch," Tadgh said with satisfaction. "You don't want to make my brother shoot. He doesn't miss. Keep the gun on me. But if you shoot me, your head will eat a bullet, I guarantee you."

"Come here, Jo," Madeline said.

Jo moved away from Stefan, inch by inch. She could hear him breathing heavily with anger. She ran toward Madeline.

They hugged at each other.

"Sorry about the stupid sex talk, Madeline. I need to improve my improvisational technique. Ciaran played along well, though." Tadgh grinned, his eyes still focused on Stefan.

Ciaran smiled slightly. "Find a better angle next time, brat. You've got a lot to learn."

"What was your code?" Jo asked.

"'Talking shit'. We've always used that one, haven't we?" Tadgh laughed.

"Nice." Jo let out a short laugh.

Ciaran waved at Stefan with his free hand. "Now, the disk, Stefan. Take it out."

Stefan pulled it out and held it in his hand.

"I really want to be fair to you, Stefan, since you worked hard for whatever it is that Juliette sent you. But Mrs. Rutherford was our family. You can't kill one of us and get away with it," Ciaran said.

"But you killed one of ours. You killed Juliette."

"No, I didn't. She might have died because of me, but I did not kill her. She was my wife."

"Mrs. Rutherford died because she called the security on me. She might have died because of me, but I didn't mean to kill her!"

"Good point. Okay, I'll let you go—but only because you're Juliette's brother. I didn't kill her, and I won't kill her family, either. But you have to leave the disk," Ciaran stated firmly.

"No," Stefan protested.

"You don't have a choice. We can keep you posted on what's in it," Tadgh added.

"I'm not a patient man, Stefan. Put the disk down and leave. There's no point dying for this. There is no crucifix or formula for you to find," said Ciaran.

They could see Stefan's body shaking with anger. He kept his grip on the disk.

They heard a shifting sound outside as if a very large bird had just taken off. Then there was a thunk on the roof and a flash of someone's legs flitting across the outside of the window, almost like the person was flying.

Madeline could see outside. A man in black, hanging from a rope, was swinging at the top of the trees. He swung past the window again and threw a small ball inside.

The ball rolled and stopped in the middle of the room. Stefan, Ciaran, and Tadgh were frozen in gun-pointing positions. None of them wanted to take their guns off of their targets.

Jo and Madeline rushed toward the ball to grab it, with the intention of throwing it outside. But before they could reach it, the ball exploded in thick red smoke.

# CHAPTER 17

The stench of rotten bodies blasted at him. Ciaran winced.

He was standing in a different world, a world he had visited many times.

Hologame.

The dark gray sky was scarred with cuts and bruises from the attack of demons' claws and fangs. Haunting trees were clumped together, and there were enough to make running difficult but not enough to form a forest.

He glanced around. Images of Madeline, Tadgh, Jo, and Stefan flickered and appeared.

Only Jo knew where they were. "Hologame," she muttered.

Ciaran strode toward Madeline and Tadgh. "Don't be alarmed. We'll be fine. It's just like playing a computer game. Except we're in it."

They still wore their normal clothes. Ciaran and Tadgh were in their long black coats. Madeline was in her long red leather jacket. Jo was in her leather pants and short furry coat.

Stefan stood by himself, confused.

None of them had their weapons.

The cold wind blew in bizarre sounds from the distance, the sound of demons calling from hell. Wolves were crying for their pack somewhere among the trees. There was the sound of running water. The water was perhaps the most familiar sound. But they couldn't see water anywhere.

"If this is a game, do we get to specify the expertise level?" Madeline asked.

"I don't think so," Jo guessed.

"If we got beaten up in here, would it be the same as on the outside?" Tadgh asked.

"Are you asking if we die in here, will we die out there? In theory, the answer is no. It's a game. But in reality, I really don't know. The designer of this game violated the rules. We didn't consent to be in here. My guess is that we're lying unconscious somewhere back there and will be eaten by wild animals by the time we get back."

"*If* we get back," Stefan sneered.

A laugh echoed behind them. Beyond the trees, a small stone bridge appeared.

Now they could see a small creek. Juliette stood on the bridge, looking magnificent. Her long red hair blew in the wind, and her bright blue eyes were clear through the thick fog.

She looked the same, Ciaran thought. But she might not be his Juliette.

"You look like Juliette," he said.

"Ten years older, though," Tadgh added.

Juliette waved her arm and sent a lightning bolt at Tadgh, hitting him and sending him flying to the ground behind him.

"I can see that you still haven't grown up. You don't mock a woman's age, Tadgh. Especially one who has total control of your environment, your life, and your death. Out there, your family can have whatever they want. But in here, in my world, you will play by my rules. You will do what I say. I alone will decide whether you live or die."

Juliette laughed. An insane laugh.

"So how do you want to play, Juliette?" Ciaran asked.

"Oh, my dear Ciaran, you're just the same as you were. Even after ten long years, you still love games, and let me guess, you still love winning."

"Who wouldn't?"

"That's exactly right. Who wouldn't want to win? So let's play the game you all wanted to play in your world. Let's play crucifix hunting. All of you against me. Here are the rules. The crucifix is in this park. You are to find it and bring it to the other end of the park for me. You will fight as a group. If you lose one person, you lose the game."

"What will happen if we lose the game?" Madeline asked.

Juliette looked at her and smiled mysteriously. "You do not want to lose, sister!"

Juliette turned around to look at Stefan.

"I thought you were dead," Stefan whispered in disbelief.

"I'm not. Win the game, and we can see each other again, brother. I'm sure you missed me."

"Why can't you tell me where it is? We don't need them," Stefan said.

"Oh, no, no! That's no fun at all. I hid it, and I traded my life for it. Now you will have to work hard to find it. Isn't that fair?" Juliette waved her arm in the air and disappeared into the darkness.

A roar of wind blew at them. "That's not wind. Wind doesn't sound like that," Tadgh said.

They looked to the sky. In the distance, a flock of half dragon-half bat creatures was flying toward them.

"Get some ammo!" Ciaran shouted.

"Tree. Tree gives life." Jo ran toward a huge tree.

"What?" Tadgh asked.

Madeline ran toward Ciaran and Jo. Stefan reluctantly followed.

Jo put her right hand on her hip. "Knife." A belt appeared, wrapping around her waist, a hunting knife in a side pocket.

"All right, so we've got the basic package. Get what you want," Ciaran instructed the others. Ciaran asked for a sword, and a gigantic sword appeared in his hand.

Tadgh, Stefan, and Madeline asked for handguns.

And suddenly, they all had guns.

The flying animals were closing in fast. Ciaran used his sword and Jo used her knife to dig into the roots of the tree, but it wouldn't budge an inch.

"Got to lose some blood here." She held the knife against her wrist.

Ciaran stopped her. "No, let me." He sliced his arm, and blood droplets fell onto the tree. Its roots pulled up like arms, revealing boxes of machine guns.

Tadgh gasped. Ciaran grabbed a gun, and everyone else followed his lead.

Ciaran and Jo pointed the machine guns to the sky and sprayed a barrage of bullets at the weird flying animals. They screamed and hissed with pain and exploded into black dust and ashes.

"Awesome!" Tadgh was enjoying this.

They heard a hiss, a shift, and a roar behind them. A leopard with horns jumped out from the bush at them. Madeline turned quickly, stood her ground, and punched it full of bullet holes.

Ciaran looked at Madeline and smiled. "Magnificent warrior."

In the distance, a dragon raised up from the ground.

Tadgh lifted his gun and took aim.

Ciaran dropped his machine gun to the ground and charged toward the dragon. "He's mine, brother. I want my blood back."

Ciaran ran, grabbed a low tree branch, and swung himself up high. He flew from one tree to another. The dragon greeted him with waves of fire. Ciaran leaped over the flames, pulled his sword, and stabbed it straight into the dragon's heart. The dragon disintegrated and crumbled to the ground. The blood that spurted from its heart was absorbed by Ciaran's hand.

When he rejoined the group, Jo gave him an admiring salute. "White Knight!"

"We have to move," Ciaran said.

They looked around, gauging their surroundings.

"She said this is a park. If it's manmade, there will likely be a lake in the middle. The trees will be surrounding it. And the hiding place will be somewhere in the center. Center of the road, middle of the lake. It has to have some kind of central logic to it," Stefan said.

"Could it be in the water?" Tadgh asked.

"Maybe. It depends," Stefan responded.

"Let's head that way to see if we can find a lake," Madeline said, pointing.

They walked for a while, and a lake appeared in front of them. They followed a path along the water, and they came upon a small island with a statue in the middle of the lake.

"That looks quite central," Jo commented.

Ciaran asked for some rope, a boat, and a waterproof weapon. He didn't get anything. "I forgot. We've got a basic package."

"I'll go out there," Stefan said and dove into the water. He reached the island, looked around, dove underneath again. He looked on top of the statue and found nothing, so he headed back to the bank of the lake. But before he could get out of the water, two long arms of a gigantic octopus wrapped around his legs to drag him down.

Madeline and Jo tried to pull him back, and Ciaran and Tadgh shot at the octopus. Bullets didn't seem to do much harm to the animal. Madeline and Jo were losing ground.

Stefan looked at Madeline. "Let go of my arm."

"No."

"Just let go, Madeline." She released him.

Stefan pulled the hunting knife out and swung at his leg. He almost passed out with the pain. The octopus was happy with what it had, however, so it went away, carrying with it Stefan's leg from the shin down.

Tadgh took his coat off and tore the fabric to stop the bleeding. "Can you keep going?" Tadgh asked.

"Do I have a choice?" Stefan winced. He was losing blood badly.

Tadgh put Stefan's arm over his shoulders and carried as much of Stefan's weight as possible.

The group kept going, searching every possible place along the lake where the crucifix could be hidden.

They approached a small bridge. They had to cross it—there was nowhere else to go on this side.

"Wait here," Ciaran said. He cautiously crossed the bridge by himself. When it seemed to be relatively safe, he came back again to escort the group over.

They soon arrived at a small temple.

"Maybe this is it," Madeline said.

"It does look like a good hiding place." Tadgh set Stefan down. "I'll have a quick check inside," Tadgh said.

"I'll look go around the back. Jo, check out the side please, and Madeline, if you could stay with Stefan?" Ciaran asked.

Tadgh cautiously pushed open the door of the temple.

Ciaran had walked around the corner, looking at the temple from the outside. Running back to the front, he yelled, "Tadgh, get out!"

But it was too late.

# CHAPTER 18

The chunky wooden door of the small temple closed Tadgh in as soon as he heard Ciaran's yelling.

"Fuck!" he muttered.

Tadgh yanked the door handle, but it wouldn't budge. He could hear the others banging from the outside, trying to knock it down.

He looked around. Nothing suspicious. He move further inside and inspected all the corners of the temple. There was no sign of the crucifix.

"Get out of the way, Tadgh!" It was Ciaran. Tadgh dove aside just before a machine gun sprayed the door and it collapsed.

As he headed toward the open doorway to leave the temple, a line of fire shot up from the floor, creating a barrier between Tadgh and the outside. The curtain of fire burned with incredible heat. The temple was small with thick brick walls and no windows. If he wasn't burned to death, he would die from lack of oxygen or smoke inhalation.

Tadgh yelled over the top of the fire. "I'm going to run through this. It's only a game, right? Should be okay."

Madeline screamed at him, "No! You'll die! You can't cross it."

She knew better. Been there and done that. She knew how much it hurt. She'd made it through the fire, but it was only because Juliette hadn't set the rules. In their current game, Juliette had set things up, and she was almost positive Tadgh couldn't cross the fire and live.

Ciaran and Jo tried every object they could find to suppress the fire for a few seconds so that Tadgh could cross. Nothing worked.

The heat inside the temple was incredible. It seemed hot enough to boil blood. The air was growing thicker and thicker. Tadgh slumped to the floor.

Madeline looked at him and knew what he was thinking. She yelled to him over the fire. "Don't cross! I'll fix this!"

But Tadgh had already lain down on the floor and didn't appear to hear what Madeline was saying to him.

Madeline ran to a nearby tree. "Tree gives life. Jo said, tree gives life. Must be some kind of game code." Madeline was thinking out loud.

She pulled out her hunting knife and cut her arms. Blood streamed onto the tree. Ciaran saw what she was doing, but he understood the reasoning behind her actions. He didn't stop her.

"Tree gives life. Okay, you have enough of my blood now, so I'm asking you to fall down and make a bridge."

Madeline pushed the tree lightly. It lifted easily from its roots and fell across the wall of fire.

Ciaran stormed inside the temple. Tadgh was no longer conscious. He carried his brother outside and lay him on the grass, Jo darted over and performed CPR. Tadgh coughed and opened his eyes. He blinked and looked up at Jo, who was sitting on top of him.

"That was smoking hot!" he managed to say teasingly.

"Thank you." Jo smiled.

The group made it to the end of the lake but still had found no crucifix.

In front of them now was something that looked like the ruins of an ancient castle. Tall stone walls with glassless arched windows towered above them. Gothic rooflines shaped like towers pointed to the bruised sky. It was a magnificent and imposing structure — in the middle of nowhere.

Juliette stepped out of the fog. "I'm disappointed. I thought you were much better than this."

"So who's going to punish us if we lose the game?" Ciaran asked.

"My game, my rules, and my execution." Juliette smiled menacingly.

"But we haven't lost yet. We still have the final round."

Juliette's grin widened. She lifted her arm up, and a sword appeared in her hand. "You asked for it, my husband."

She swung her sword at Ciaran. He blocked with his. The clash of metal against metal sang in the air. The force of the contact pushed Ciaran a few steps backward.

Ciaran could see the shadow of dragon wings behind Juliette. Each blow of her sword carried an incredible amount of supernatural force. She was cheating.

Ciaran swung and attacked her, pushing her back several steps. His sword, however, was obviously inferior to hers.

Madeline asked Jo. "What kind of sword does he need to win?"

"One soaked in angel blood."

"What does that mean? I don't have angel's blood." She ran to a tree. She cut her hand again. "Here is my blood. I need that sword."

Nothing.

Still engrossed in their swordfight, Juliette gave Ciaran a hard kick, sending him down to his knees. In this hologame world, gender held no power and gave no advantage. Only the power of the game mattered. Ciaran knew that.

He had power, but his weapon was inferior. His sword had already been chipped and would break soon.

Tadgh grabbed his knife and rushed forward. He hit hard against an invisible wall and slumped to the ground.

"Game rules, Tadgh. Their fight is one-on-one. You can't get in," Jo said.

"But that bitch has a better weapon. How is that fair?"

Jo darted toward the tree where Madeline was still trying to get the sword. "Nothing yet?" Jo asked.

"No, I've given my blood. What else can I do?"

Jo took her own knife and cut herself. "Here is my blood, too. We give you our sister blood. Pure blood. Pure love. Give us strength. Give us the sword."

There was a rumble from within the tree trunk. Then it opened, revealing a knight's sword with a blood red blade.

Madeline grabbed the sword and ran toward Ciaran and Juliette.

Before Jo could warn her, she heard the thunk of Madeline hitting the wall as Tadgh did.

"I can't get in!" she yelled. "Jo, what do I do?"

"Ciaran has to ask for it himself. You can't bring the sword to him."

Ciaran's sword broke in half, and he tossed it away.

Juliette laughed. "Well, my warrior. I don't want you to be disadvantaged."

She opened her palm, and her sword disappeared.

They now fought hand to hand.

Juliette's arms were as hard as steel, and her strength was superhuman. As soon as she made contact with him, Ciaran knew her game strength was abnormal. She was cheating again. He wondered if she had been all along and not a single moment between them had been genuine.

His lack of concentration caused him to take a few blows from Juliette's steely arms. Whatever this was in front of him was a monster, not a woman.

*Concentrate. Look into her eyes,* he told himself. She was a monster. And he was White Knight. It was his mission to destroy all evil.

Ciaran clenched his fists and went head-on with Juliette. He blocked her steel blows with his kicks. The sheer force of will from him was something she could not defeat.

Ciaran pounded on her. Blows and kicks until she fell, tumbling across the ground. He wouldn't stop until he defeated this evil force.

He charged.

Ciaran could see Madeline holding the sword outside the fighting arena. He knew what she had done to get it.

He continued his attack on the woman. She roared with a demonic thunder of anger and frustration. Her power was abating. From the ground, she looked up at Ciaran, who was walking toward her to finish the job.

She looked at him with Juliette's eyes.

Those innocent, bright eyes he had loved years ago. Was this Juliette he was about to kill? It couldn't be. But how could a demon have her eyes?

She started humming the tune of the song she had written on their honeymoon, the song she sang before she died. "Little hummingbird, do you see the sky? It is free. It is yours. Fly. Past the mountains. Past the oceans. There. You will find love . . ."

Kneeling on the ground, Juliette looked at him with tearful eyes containing a sea of innocence, those he had fallen for when they first met at Oxford University. She had died for him. How could he now execute her?

That single moment of hesitation was what Juliette had been waiting for.

She flexed and turned her fist. It morphed into a blade which she stabbed straight into Ciaran's body.

He heard Madeline scream as he fell. *Is this the end?* he wondered.

He couldn't kill Juliette, regardless of what she did to him.

As Juliette withdrew her steel arm from him, Ciaran slumped to the ground.

Juliette raised up with a devil's smile. "Ever lost a game, Ciaran?"

"I don't like losing, and I've never lost."

"So this will be your first loss. Your first, and your last." Juliette extended her arm, and her sword returned.

She was going to kill Ciaran.

From the ground, Ciaran looked up at a demon.

"You're not Juliette!"

Ciaran reached up. The sword in Madeline's hands vibrated and then flew toward Ciaran. He grabbed it and swung quickly, beheading the woman in front of him.

She screamed even as her head fell from her shoulders. Then her entire body shattered like crystal and vanished into thin air.

Ciaran muttered, "If you were Juliette, you would know that I lost my first game to her. The *real* Juliette. Demon bitch!"

# CHAPTER 19

Tadgh winced as the cold moisture from the ground seeped into his skin. He opened his eyes groggily and immediately registered the reality of the situation. He scrambled to reach for his gun and saw the muzzle of Stefan's pointing at his face.

"Hey, hey, stay still," Stefan said.

Tadgh quickly took inventory of the scene as he stood up. They were back at the rest stop. Madeline and Jo had just gotten up. Ciaran was still on the ground.

Stefan limped badly, but he managed to reach over and grab Madeline. He pointed the gun at her.

"Without Ciaran, no one can work on your disk, Stefan," Tadgh said. "And he doesn't look as if he's coming back soon."

"I can see that," Stefan scolded. "Here's my solution. I'll take Madeline with me. When our White Knight here wakes up, he and Jo will decode the disk for me. Then we'll talk again."

"Let me try again. I'll go with you," Jo said.

"No, it's better you stay with Ciaran and Tadgh. I can handle this, Jo," Madeline told her.

"Hear that, Jo? Your big sister wants you to do your job and be a good girl." Stefan smirked.

"When we sort out the disk, how can we find you?" Tadgh asked.

Stefan laughed. "Why don't you just come right out and ask where I'm hiding?" he mocked. "I'll contact you. Remember, I like Madeline, but I like what's in the disk much more. Don't disappoint me."

Stefan pulled Madeline out the door.

Jo stomped her feet on the floor. "Damn it!"

"Careful—you'll punch holes on the floor with those heels. Damaging national park property will land us in jail."

Jo glared at Tadgh. "That's not funny."

"I'm not trying to be funny. But I have to entertain us somehow because we're going to be here for hours."

"Why?"

Tadgh nodded at Ciaran. "He'll be out for that long."

Jo looked at Ciaran. "Because of the stab wound?" Jo ripped Ciaran's shirt open and saw a large red scar where the demon had stabbed him.

"You're just checking out his abs, aren't you?"

"What's your problem, Tadgh? Why you keep making stupid comments?"

Tadgh crouched so that his eyes were level with Jo's. "It's because I'm feeling completely stupid right now. We did everything we could to rescue you. And then things got so messed up. People we care for died. Now we got you back. And he took Madeline. When will this end? How many more people will be killed?"

"You care for Madeline."

"Not as much he does." Tadgh pointed at Ciaran. "In fact, I don't think I've seen him care that much for anyone in years. Now he's out, and I couldn't even keep Madeline safe for him." Tadgh shook his head.

"You couldn't help it. Stefan is a trained soldier. He had a gun on you."

"So you're saying I was scared shitless when he pointed the gun at me?"

"Why do you have twist everything I say the wrong way? What did I do to offend you?" Jo jabbed her finger at Tadgh's chest.

He shook his head. "It's just me. I'm sorry."

Ciaran stirred.

Tadgh tapped his shoulder. "Okay, get up Ciaran."

"Why does he take such a long time to wake up?"

"He's allergic to anesthesia. It must have been in the smoke bomb they threw at us. It knocks him out for hours. And it'll get worse."

"How?" Jo asked and picked up the sleeve that contained the disk from the ground. It was empty. She showed it to Tadgh.

"Shit!" he exclaimed.

"Okay, so we have no disk. Stefan thought we had it. I don't know what to do now. Who were those men with the red bombs?" Jo said.

"Probably the same ones who attacked us at Robert's house just before we came here. They burned his house down and killed his wife and daughter." He searched Ciaran's jacket pocket. "Holy fuck . . . Juliette's diary is gone, too." Tadgh pulled at his hair as if it would help him find a solution.

Jo's eyes teared up.

"Oh, no, that's the last thing I need here. Girl crying."

"I don't cry." Jo ground her teeth. "I'm female, and this is a normal biological reaction of the female body in situations of distress."

Tadgh stared. "Why can't you just say girls cry when they're stressed?" he grumbled. "Never mind."

Ciaran opened his eyes. He was too groggy to make any sense of what was going on. Tadgh pulled him up.

"All right, let's go." Tadgh pulled Ciaran's arm over his shoulders to help him walk. Ciaran pushed him away.

"All right, all right. I've got it. You don't have to carry me."

Tadgh released him, and Ciaran slumped to the floor again.

"I'm going to help you whether you like it or not." Tadgh pulled his arm over his shoulders again and started walking.

"Back to the car, this way," Tadgh said, steering his brother.

Ciaran pulled away from him, and ran to a tree and vomited violently.

Tadgh looked at Jo. "That's what I meant by it gets worse. He does that all the time. And if you ever tell him you've seen him like that, you'll never be his friend!"

Jo rolled her eyes. "Men and their dicks!"

"Excuse me?"

"You wanted me to put things simply. Or would you rather me analyze the neurological system of the male species when it comes to their so-called sexual organs?"

"No, thank you. Let me keep my sanity."

When Ciaran had emptied the contents of his stomach, his brother half dragged, half carried him to the car. He put Ciaran in the backseat and got behind the wheel.

Tadgh sat for a long moment, staring at the dashboard.

"Out of gas?" Jo asked.

"I can't believe I have to drive this stupid machine!"

"You don't know how to drive?"

"Of course I do, excuse me! But I drive normal cars like normal people. Not this piece of shit."

"This is a very expensive sports car. It's supposed to be every man's wet dream."

"Well, it's not my dream, okay?"

"I can drive," Jo offered.

"Oh, no, thank you. You Americans drive on the wrong side of the road. This is not a hologame. If we die here, it's going to be very real!"

"We Americans think you British drive on the wrong side of the road."

"Stop babbling and let me concentrate."

Tadgh focused and started the car while Jo rolled her eyes and swallowed a laugh.

The car jerked, roared up, accelerated, stopped, and stalled.

"Don't tell me—you drive an automatic."

"Just shut up." Tadgh tried again, and this time he succeeded. They made it to the highway.

"You might get a ticket for driving too slow."

"Just shut up."

# CHAPTER 20

The stuffy air of a small hotel room greeted Madeline and Stefan as soon as he opened the door. "Sorry, it's all I could find on such short notice. The location is the best, though," Stefan said and shoved her into the room.

He locked the door and limped toward the only bed in the room. He flopped onto it, wincing with pain. He pulled his jeans up to the knee, and saw a bright red scar around his leg where he had chopped it off in the hologame. The scar was swollen and looked infected.

"Fucking stupid game," he mumbled to himself.

Madeline walked over. Stefan immediately grabbed his gun.

"I just want to have a look at your injury. Are you going to hold me at gunpoint all night long? We used to be friends, Stefan."

"You're good with words, Madeline. But you need to check the dictionary for the definition of friendship."

If this continued, getting away from Stefan would be difficult, Madeline mused. She glanced at his wound. "It's badly infected. You might need medical treatment. If it gets any worse, you'll lose your leg for real."

"I'll take care of this little scratch."

"You can't do what you want to do if you can't walk. I won't be able to carry you, even metaphorically."

"I said I'll figure it out."

"All right then. I have to give it to you, though. Chopping your leg off was very brave, even if it was just in a game."

Stefan smiled slightly. "I can do a lot better than that."

"I bet."

There was a knock on the door. Stefan grabbed the gun. They waited, and an envelope was slipped under the door. Stefan waited another moment and then picked up the envelope.

He opened the envelope to find a fancy card. He glanced at the card and gave it to Madeline. "For you," he said.

The card read:

*"Dear Madeline,*

*It is my pleasure to invite you to visit our residence. I trust you will find this meeting beneficial. We had a brief encounter earlier. Thus you know the resources I can provide to help you to achieve what you want. Should you accept the invitation, your transportation is ready now.*

*Sincerely yours, Mr. Kelley.*

*P.S. Your friend Stefan may accompany you. Should he keep you against your will or cause you any harm, I assure you he will not make it out of that hotel alive."*

She gave the note back to Stefan, trying to look as smug as she could. She had nothing to lose. Being captured here or there. She remembered the encounter at Robert's place. The men had drawn their guns on her but hadn't fired.

*Who is her ally?*

"Friendly and helpful people, aren't they?" Madeline said.

"Who are they?"

"I have no idea. They sent about fifteen men to burn down a house, and they killed four people, including two innocent bystanders and a woman and her baby. So I guess they'll give you the same if you stop me from accepting their invitation. If you can call it an invitation."

"So you want to go?"

"Well, both you and they have pointed guns at me. What do you think I'm going to do?"

Madeline grabbed her jacket and left the room. Stefan followed like a meek dog. As they walked along the sidewalk, a car approached them and stopped. The uniformed driver spoke to Madeline. "Ms. Madeline Roux?"

"Yes?"

He gestured toward the car. "Your transport, ma'am."

Madeline nodded toward Stefan. "He's with me."

"Yes, ma'am."

They arrived at a private villa outside London. The house sat back almost a mile from the road and was surrounded by nothing but green fields. It looked like a converted barn. She was sure it held a world of surprises inside.

The door swung open as they approached and text images floated in the air. "Welcome."

"You can't afford a screen? Or a voice announcement? I don't want to walk into your *words*," Madeline said.

They entered a large foyer. A robotic voice directed, "Please sit. Someone will be with you shortly."

For a moment, it seemed oddly quiet. Then the air thickened, and Madeline knew what it was. It was the holocast she'd experienced at the museum.

"Mr. Kelley, if you're there, I'd like to talk to you. After all, you're the one who summoned us here."

A hologram of a man in his sixties appeared. He was sitting on the sofa opposite Madeline and Stefan.

"Welcome back to the family, Madeline."

"Thank you. But I'm happy with who I am now— and with the people I'm with."

"Family is important."

"Well, I've had a decent life without having family. I have no plans to change that."

"I'm sorry you've been down here all this time by yourself. But thirty-three years is long enough. It's time to come back."

A chill shot up her spine.

Fear crossed her mind. Did her age coincide with the number that had bothered Ciaran and his family so much? She decided it was purely coincidental because she didn't even know the exact date she was born. Someone had dumped her in a basket and left her on the doorstep of a stranger when she was only four weeks old. But even age was a speculation. She hadn't said anything to Ciaran.

Based on the note this man had sent her, he had organized the attack at Robert's place and had sent them into the hologame with the demonic version of Juliette.

This man had some kind of connection to Juliette. And now it seemed he had ties with her as well. In addition, he'd confirmed she was thirty-three years of age. If she still believed all of this was just coincidental, she would have to be an idiot.

"Madeline!" Stefan called.

"Huh?"

"You okay?"

She nodded and turned toward the man. "Who are you?"

"I'm Richard Kelley, your grandfather. Your parents died in a battle, and you were stolen from them."

"A battle?"

"A battle between us and our enemies. We don't live on Earth."

"So you're alien?" Stefan muffled a laugh and became quiet when he received a cold stare from the old man.

"We're human. We just took residence in a place that is far more supreme than this filthy, polluted, and overpopulated planet."

"What do you want from me, apart from a family reunion?" Madeline asked.

"The crucifix. The sample gold inside the crucifix, to be precise."

"The crucifix has been where it is for a long time. Why do you want it now?" Madeline asked.

"The thirty-three-year cycle is very important to us. Your parents fought and died in that battle. We never regained our strength after that. And now, the critical time is back again, and if we don't have the gold, we will be destroyed forever."

"I'm only a journalist. What can I possibly do to help you fight battles that aren't even my own?"

"I'm certainly not going to fight any of your battles, wherever they are!" Stefan raised his voice.

"Your father was my ally. It was a shame he passed away because of the mishaps of Juliette. But we continued his work."

"What the hell are you talking about?"

"Your father was going to tell you his plan for you. But he didn't have a chance. Apparently, he didn't tell you much beforehand."

"I don't care about any of this, and I have no intention of being friends with you." Stefan stood up.

"Because you want the gold, you kill women and children, and burn down houses?" Madeline asked.

"Collateral damage . . ."

"Who the hell do you think you are? Collateral damage? They were innocent people!" Madeline stood, enraged.

"I regret it, but it couldn't be helped. As I said, Juliette is the key to our technology. I can't let anyone get their hands on any trace of her material—including the disk and the diary."

"She's my sister! So fuck your technology, fuck your people, and fuck your gold. I'm done with this." Stefan grabbed Madeline and turned to leave.

"When your father retrieved Juliette, she was effectively a corpse. He lost his life because of that. I can only revive a part of Juliette's mind, and to fulfill your father's dying wish, we need to get the crucifix which is somewhere in Fountains Abbey. Don't you want to fight for your father's legacy, Stefan?"

Stefan and Madeline looked out the door. Dozens of men in black were lurking.

"What exactly do you want from me?" Stefan asked.

"I came in peace. I just wanted to meet my granddaughter. Besides, I'm going to help you get the crucifix, and you can keep it."

Stefan narrowed his eyes. "And what do you want in return?"

"I only ask for a sample. You can keep the rest. It's a win-win solution, and a very generous offer from our end."

"Why can't you just ask Juliette where the crucifix is?"

"Her mind is very unstable. We get very limited information from her. The most I can do is simulate her image — the one you saw in the hologame."

So Richard had no idea Juliette had spoken to her at the chapel, Madeline thought. And he certainly didn't know about the warning that the crucifix killed. Maybe she should just play along and help Stefan obtain the crucifix.

"What support will you give me?" Stefan asked.

"You will have my men. They are well-trained and well-equipped."

Stefan nodded. "That should do for now. When can we start?"

"Our people are ready to go as soon as you're ready. We just need to wait until my people finish decoding Juliette's disk. I want to be sure there is no additional information we need to know in order to plan accordingly. Once that's confirmed, you're good to go."

"The disk?" Madeline asked.

"Yes, my men took the disk and the diary from you while you were out and about in your hologame world. You think I sent you to the game for fun? It was a practice round for your show and a test of your skills. Apparently you both passed."

"Test for what?"

"You're our family. You're a warrior, Madeline. But you were stuck on this planet for a long time. I've got to make sure you can be trained. You can't be a part of us if the only skill you have is cooking."

"I don't cook. But I can kill. I believe you know that," Madeline muttered.

"Indeed." The old man laughed. "One other thing. You can't go back to the LeBlancs after this is done."

"Why not?" Madeline was astonished.

"We're not exactly on friendly terms with them and haven't been for generations. So if you're involved with them, you cannot be with us."

"Then I don't want any of this." She turned to leave.

The grandfather cleared his throat. "If you don't want this family, that is fine. However, you know quite a bit of our plans, so I'm afraid I'll have to hold you until things are finished. If you ruin our plan—and I hope you don't—I won't leave the LeBlanc boys alive."

If she refused, they would keep her, and Ciaran would try to find her. Ciaran was in the dark about all this. But if she agreed, then she would have control over the situation and could communicate with Ciaran to ensure he didn't get involved in the crucifix hunt.

Once things were over, she could go back to Ciaran and break her promise with this Kelley family. Considering this a good plan, she nodded. "All right, I'll stay and help. Don't hurt any of the LeBlancs," Madeline said.

The grandfather smiled warmly. "Good news for the whole family! Remember, Madeline, don't take your promise lightly. If you return to the LeBlancs after this, I'll hunt you down wherever you are, no matter how long it takes."

She couldn't let Ciaran walk blindly into this trap trying to find her.

"Do I have your word?" the grandfather asked.

"Yes," Madeline said.

Stefan laughed in disbelief. "So Ciaran gets nothing! Absolutely nothing! I'm excited now. When can we begin this hunting game?

"Tomorrow at the latest."

The holocast disappeared.

# CHAPTER 21

Ciaran used the computer in his bedroom instead of the one in his office. He needed to be here, in this corner of the house. He stared at the screen, not knowing where to start his search. This had never happened before.

This master suite was in the new part of the house, and it was supposed to have been a new start to his life. This room was where he had begun his connection with Madeline, the woman who made him think he could love again.

And now, she was gone.

The wait was torturous, and he needed all the time he could get. He didn't have the disk. He couldn't make anything up because he had no idea what Juliette had put on it. When Stefan called to bargain for Madeline's life, he would have nothing to offer.

He sat, brooding. It was very unlike him.

But he knew a dangerous storm was heading his way. He didn't know what kind of storm it would be. But this time, he would be defeated.

Stefan called. Ciaran frowned at the number. It was too soon. He needed more time. But he needed Stefan's confirmation that Madeline was okay. He answered.

"Hello, there. I've got some good news, and I can't wait until tomorrow to let you know." Stefan's smugness oozed out of receiver.

"Say it quickly, Stefan. I'm expecting a phone call," Ciaran snapped.

"Okay, then. I—no, *we*—have some new developments on our end and would like to let you know that you don't have to bother with the disk anymore."

"What do you mean by that?"

"There's no need to play games with me anymore, Ciaran. You don't have the disk, do you?"

Ciaran didn't know what to say. His brain was simply not working at the moment.

Stefan continued. "Madeline and I have some news for you."

He felt sweat running down his spine. "I'll only hear it from Madeline. Put her on the phone."

Stefan laughed. "She's in the bathroom right now. I'll get her for you. But the exciting news is that she found her grandfather."

"That's great news. But I can't imagine it would make you very excited."

"Crucifix aside, I do like her, you know. Her grandfather is going to help us find the crucifix and the gold. Madeline is happy, and I'm happy, too. Thing is, her grandfather doesn't like you much. I tried to put in a good word for you. I really did. But he forbade Madeline to come back to you."

"Put Madeline on the phone."

"Sure. Oh, and just between us men, he said he'd kill her if you come near her. So if you care for her, my advice is to leave her alone."

Fury rolled over him in waves. "Brag on, Stefan. You know I won't believe a thing you say."

"My bad, but I'm not bragging! I'm willing to forgive you for killing my sister. I did kill a few people on your end. So let's call it even. Let bygones be bygones. You don't have to worry about the crucifix, about Madeline, about the disk, or about anything else for that matter . . ."

"Put Madeline on the phone, or I will hang up."

Stefan clucked his tongue. "Richard Kelly has an army of people. He's been waiting for thirty-three years, and he's not going to let Madeline go that easily. She's important to him, just as my sister is important to me. Somehow you ended up with both women. But your time is up. You're done, Ciaran."

Ciaran's blood ran cold. He gripped the letter opener so hard that it cut into his hand. Blood dripped on the piece of elegant white paper in front of him.

Stefan's voice suddenly became cheery. "Here she is!"

"Hello," Madeline's sultry voice came across. "Hello? Who is this? Grandfather? Who am I talking to, Stefan?"

"It's me, Madeline."

There was silence on the other end of the phone.

"Ciaran . . . how . . . how are you?"

"Have you found your grandfather?"

"No, he found me. I . . . I didn't know anything about him before."

"How old are you? You should know that answer."

"I . . ."

"It's not a trick question, Madeline."

"Thirty-three, but I can explain."

"Did he threaten you?"

An instant message signaled an alert sound. Ciaran switched the screen. The message said, *"Spot the hotel, Lindsay."*

"I know where you are now, Madeline. I can come and get you right now."

"No."

"I know he's threatened you, but I . . ."

"No. I said no, Ciaran."

"I can help you and your grandfather find the crucifix. If that's what you want . . ."

"I don't need you, Ciaran. We can take care of it. I don't need you at all. Bye, Ciaran."

Madeline hung up.

He stood looking out the window for a long moment, trying to make sense of what just happened. He wanted to throw his phone at the wall. But he didn't. What good would it do?

He walked back and forth in the room, thinking. He leaned against his desk. He wasn't sure how long he stood there before he heard footsteps in the hallway. Tadgh, Jo, and the cat Migi appeared at the door.

Ciaran smiled at Jo.

"Jo has an idea. Given that Stefan has never seen the contents of the disk, she could make up a . . ." Tadgh trailed off when he saw the blank stare on Ciaran's face.

"Ahh . . . any news?" Tadgh asked.

Ciaran shrugged. "It's over, Tadgh."

"What do you mean?"

"Madeline said she found her grandfather and will use his help to find the crucifix herself. She won't be needing us anymore. Jo, I can make arrangements for you to go back to New York."

"I . . . can I talk to her, Ciaran?" Jo asked.

"I'm sure you can. But you'll have to call her yourself. She finished her conversation with me. Now if you'll both excuse me, I have some work to see to."

"Of course. I'll talk to you later. Let's go, Jo."

❀ ❀ ❀

Tadgh dragged Jo away from Ciaran's room and strode downstairs. "You said you'd teach me how to play computer games, right?" Tadgh asked.

"Sure," Jo raised an eyebrow.

"Let's go to the game room. Ciaran's got truckloads of them."

They entered the game room. Rows of computers were lined up in the room, all different sizes and models. Tadgh gestured widely. "See? All ours. We're free now. We have nothing to do. Let's play!"

Jo chose the most basic computer. "What do you want to play? Tennis, ping-pong, car racing?"

"I want to fight."

Jo showed Tadgh how to play some basic fighting games, then they role played in a game.

In the game, Tadgh pounded at Jo. "Wow, you're too aggressive for a beginner!"

"It's a game, right? I wouldn't do that in real life." Then he picked up the weapons in the game and fought like a mad man, killing all the other characters, including Jo's.

On the computer screen, a triumphant jingle came out with the words, "Congratulations, you won!"

Tadgh stood up, pulled the keyboard out, and whacked at the computer monitor. "Win, my ass." He pounded the computer until it was just a pile of scrap metal. Finally, he slumped to the floor, breathing heavily.

Jo waited, then she went over and hugged him. "Okay, there now, tell me what's going on."

Tadgh sat on the floor, leaning against the wall. "Just shoot me!"

"You broke the computer. Want to play a more advanced game?"

Tadgh put his head between his knees. "Oh shit!"

Jo waited patiently.

"I've only seen my brother like that once. After Juliette died. He didn't have the answer—and still doesn't—about her death. It was painful for him. But when he finally accepted her death, he looked just like that."

"If she's dead, and he accepted it, isn't that a good thing?"

"It was. But the other night when he thought he would lose Madeline, he wouldn't accept it. He would fight for her. He'd never accept defeat."

"You mean he loves her."

"I don't think he'd use the 'L' word."

"So what's wrong with him?"

"He thinks he's responsible for Juliette's death. We all knew she just used him. But he still wants to believe they had a fairy tale, that she at least loved him for real at one time."

"Okay, once bitten, twice shy. He doesn't think he can use the 'L' word with Madeline. And now Madeline's told him she doesn't need him. I know that hurts. But it's not worth you destroying all of these very innocent computers."

"I think Madeline loves him, too."

"Only need half a brain and one eye to see that, Tadgh. I'm not stupid. I saw that in the hologame."

Tadgh yanked at his hair. "Madeline believes the crucifix kills. It has explosives, poison, or something in it. She wasn't going to let Ciaran go anywhere near it. But Ciaran is stubborn. If you tell him that the crucifix has explosives in it, he's definitely going to go looking for it. So if I were Madeline, I'd do my best to *help* Stefan find the crucifix so he can blow *himself* up."

"How did you come to that conclusion?"

"She told me about the crucifix. I think the whole grandfather deal was bogus. The fact that she's not coming back here, maybe it's part of a deal she has with Stefan. That guy is a nasty piece of shit."

"So why can't we tell Ciaran and try to figure the whole thing out? We can't let Madeline do it on her own."

"I promised her I wouldn't tell. I also want to keep my brother out of danger."

"You know what Tadgh, if I were Ciaran, I would beat you up." Jo stood up and marched out of the room.

Tadgh trailed behind submissively and asked, "Where are you going?"

"I'm telling Ciaran. And if you don't like it, bite me!"

## CHAPTER 22

The real Fountains Abbey greeted Madeline with the magnificence of a place that had housed hundreds of monks who lived and died there centuries ago. Located in the endless and mysterious national park, the history and the beauty of the place attracted so many tourists that searching for a crucifix during the daytime hours was almost impossible.

"Can you ask your men to be a little less conspicuous? All they need are dark sunglasses and people will pick them out as member of the mafia," Madeline complained.

"They're not *my* men," Stefan said between his teeth, glancing at the five fighters Richard had sent along with them.

They walked down to the valley from the visitor center and recognized the grounds. It was the setting from the hologame they had played the day before.

Madeline looked around—miles of trees, a gigantic manmade lake, and the ruined sites of abbeys and graveyards.

"This is just great. We may have to spend a lifetime here, digging," Stefan muttered.

"We need more information," Madeline said.

She turned around, asking Douglas, the head of the group, "Is there anything we can do to speed this up?"

Douglas shook his head.

"Can we at least have a dog to scent something out?" Stefan asked.

"We have a scanner," Douglas offered. "Would that help?"

"A scanner for what? Metals? Explosives?"

"It doesn't detect. It just provides visuals of objects up to six feet underground."

"Great, I'm looking forward to scanning the graveyard," Madeline muttered. "We'll start at the far end of the lake and work our way up to the abbeys. There are too many tourists in the abbeys right now.

They'd be alarmed if we looked like we were scanning for a bomb."

The group walked along the lake's edge to approach the park at the far end. Halfway there, they saw Ciaran, Tadgh, and Jo on the other side.

"Just great. They sniffed this out already," Stefan moaned.

All the men had their hands in their pockets, ready for necessary action. Madeline knew they were packing the dart guns.

"No fighting," she said. "No need to fight. None of you will draw a weapon here. Let me talk to them." Madeline approached the narrow, railing-less bridge that led over the water. At the other side, Ciaran approached. They both accessed the bridge but kept their distance from one another.

"Madeline." Ciaran nodded an aloof greeting. His raven black hair was tied back, revealing that face graced by God that she had fallen for at first sight. His smoky gray eyes no longer looked at her with passion but with calculated strategies. His hands were shoved his pockets as if he was about to negotiate with an adversary that he considered lesser than him.

"You don't own this park, do you?"

"No, it's a public place. A very beautiful historic site that anyone with an appreciation for history and nature can visit."

"And that's what you're doing here?"

"Of course. Jo is going back to New York soon. It would be a shame if she missed seeing this site. She might not have a chance to come back. We would love it to become one of her fond memories."

*Damn his fancy words and damn his fancy accent,* Madeline thought.

Ciaran gazed at her. The intensity in his eyes was so strong she thought it could punch holes through her body. There were so many questions in them. Questions that had neither been asked nor answered.

Hadn't last night's conversation been uncomfortable enough? Did he have to cause more pain? What had Tadgh told him? He'd promised he wouldn't open his mouth. But here was Ciaran, standing right in front of her. So best guess, Tadgh had spilled the beans.

Ciaran was here, searching for the crucifix like everybody else. She didn't think he'd go for the gold. Rather, he was looking for an answer about Juliette. If Tadgh had told him about the possible danger of the crucifix, then that would motivate him even more.

"I have friends with me as well." Madeline gestured toward the fighters. "So I'm playing the tour guide."

"I see."

A small group of visitors went past.

"It's a big place. There are a lot of things to see here," Madeline continued.

Ciaran stepped forward. Madeline stepped backward.

"Madeline, we don't have all day. Our friends are 'dying' to see the entire site here," Stefan called out.

Ciaran stepped forward. Madeline backed down off the bridge.

"Don't." She grunted out the word to Ciaran between her teeth. The fighters moved in.

"Ciaran, we're late. Let's go. The party is waiting at home," Tadgh yelled out.

Ciaran grinned. "I invited you to our party, but you declined. If you change your mind, our home is always open for you, Madeline."

Two tourists walked past.

"That's enough, Madeline. We're very late. Our friends need to get home. Their families are waiting." Stefan grabbed her arm.

Madeline could see Ciaran's eyes burning with anger. But he said nothing more. Another group of tourists walked past the bridge.

"Ciaran, I have to go . . ."

Ciaran reached out for her elbow. She saw the men with their hands at their back pockets.

"No." She glared at them, warning them. "Please let go, Ciaran."

"All you have to do is to say you've changed your mind, and I'll take you home right now," he growled.

"Hey!" Stefan came over and shoved Ciaran back. "Don't you touch her. She said no."

"She said no to those scumbags over there to stop them from pulling their weapons out in a public place," Ciaran snarled back.

"You think I won't?" Stefan grabbed Ciaran's collar. Ciaran grabbed him back.

"Don't, you two." Madeline pulled Stefan back. Another group of tourists ambled past. Stefan grumbled some profanity.

"I want you to leave, Ciaran. Please."

"You hear that? She doesn't want you anymore." Stefan sneered.

Ciaran moved one step forward and swung a punch right at the side of Stefan's face, knocking him to the ground. Five men pulled their weapons, and Madeline jumped front of Ciaran. "Put your weapons away. I'm in charge. I'll tell my grandfather."

Stefan stood up and looked about to charge at Ciaran.

"No, Stefan," she said then turned around, looking at Ciaran. "How much more do you want to punish me, Ciaran?"

"I don't . . ."

"Then go, please."

Ciaran looked at her one last time, then left. She wasn't sure who was hurting more when they parted, but she had to move on and finish this.

There was a killer crucifix to find.

She shoved her hands into the pockets of her leather jacket, and they hit something.

"You lose something?" Stefan frowned, looking at the expression on her face.

"No. I just need some tissues." She sniffled.

Stefan rolled his eyes and walked toward the fighters. "Anyone have any tissue?"

# CHAPTER 23

A moment later, Ciaran drove out of the national park, headed toward Mortlake. Both Tadgh and Jo sat in the back seat.

Ciaran glanced at Tadgh in the mirror. "Okay, if you have anything on your mind, speak now."

"You couldn't refrain from punching Stefan? What if those guys had actually shot at you?" Tadgh scolded.

"They didn't."

"Is that all you have to say? I thought I was the reckless one in this family!" Tadgh exclaimed.

"It's done. There's no point arguing about it. Where did you plant the bug, Ciaran?" Jo asked.

"In Madeline's pocket. I slipped her a pocket knife, too."

Tadgh shook his head. "Why didn't you give her a gun?"

"The biggest compromise I made was to agree to go along with you two and let Madeline handle this by herself. I can't offer more than that."

Tadgh grumbled some profanity and then shut up, looking out the window.

Mrs. Hanson's house still wore the police security banners. Apparently, nothing much had been done here by the police since their last visit. Ciaran walked straight in, peeling the police seal off.

"Are you going to be okay going in there?" Tadgh asked Jo, concern filling his eyes. Jo smiled, and her green cat eyes almost glittered.

"Very sweet of you to think of me, Tadgh. But Stefan didn't do anything in here that traumatized me. Plus, I don't get scared easily."

Ciaran looked around, pulling some projectors and leftover computer equipment together.

"How did Stefan have it set it up, Jo?"

"He didn't exactly set anything up here. He gave me a piece of junk called a computer and asked me to decode the disk. I think he knew this was a communication center for whoever he was working for, but he really had no idea how to operate it."

Ciaran nodded and concentrated on a couple of broken wires.

"What medium do you think they're using?" asked Jo.

"The most primitive holocast model uses sound frequency. Why don't we try that?"

"You think we can get a frequency in here?" Tadgh asked.

Ciaran nodded. Jo approached a computer. "I'll work on this one," she said and sat down in front of the monitor. Tadgh stood behind, rocking back and forth from his heels to his toes. Ciaran put in the code, and the computer screen popped up an authorization box.

"Okay," Jo smiled. "Stefan always asked me to type in this key he had written on a piece of paper. 524HJUP12.653.212.OZR."

The computer flashed, "Authorized."

"How did you remember that?" Tadgh asked.

"Photographic memory." Jo grinned.

"Did you get it working for Stefan?" Tadgh asked.

"No! I always seemed to call up a wrong authorisation box for Stefan. What a shame!"

"All right. Let's start the search," Ciaran said and took over computer duty. A while later, there was a diagram on the computer monitor and a needle hitched up. "That's it!" Ciaran said and pointed at the diagram.

Both Ciaran and Jo typed lines of codes and commands into the computer.

"Stupid lightwaves," Ciaran muttered, more to himself than to anyone else.

A moment later, Jo yelped in delight.

And then, "Got you, bitch," Ciaran muttered.

Tadgh cocked an eyebrow, amused by the fact that Ciaran did not realize that he was streaming profanity as he worked.

They heard static on the speaker. Then a robotic female voice spoke. "Verification affirmative. Ciaran LeBlanc. This is TK5467.23.7 channel authorized by Sciphil Central."

"Sounds friendly," Tadgh said.

"I'd like to talk to Sciphil Two," Ciaran directed.

"Sciphil Two is not available. I am authorized to give you necessary assistance."

"Last week, there was a troop helping me at the creek in Henley on Thames. Did Sciphil Two send them?"

"Affirmative."

"Can I have access to them?"

"Affirmative. How many do you need?"

"As many as you can give."

"The direct contact will be sent to you. This channel can only be used for three minutes, Earth time. What is the next task?"

"Earth time? Where are you exactly?" Tadgh asked.

"Aphiemi, AKA Aphi, satellite station of Eudaiz."

"How far from here?" Jo said.

"We're not in the same dimension. There is no available data on physical distances."

Ciaran nodded. "Dimensional travel," he muttered. Then he asked, "The people attacking us were using dart guns that could turn organic objects into thin air. Any idea who they are and where they come from?"

"That weapon is used exclusively by the Kelleys."

Ciaran paused. "What's the relationship between Madeline Roux and the Kelleys?"

The computer monotoned the answer. "Madeline Kelley, age thirty-three, the only daughter of Thomas Kelley and Diana Kelley. Lost on planet at four weeks of age. Recently found by grandfather Richard Kelley . . ."

"Yet she doesn't have green skin and a big malformed head," Tadgh said.

"You are referring to extraterrestrial creatures in your dimension. Eudaizian's complexion is . . ."

"That's enough." Ciaran cut the computer off. "Is Juliette one of yours?"

"Please elaborate on the term *yours*."

"Is she like Madeline?"

"Negative."

"So she is human?"

"Negative."

"Damnit, so what is she?"

"Please elaborate on the term *damnit*."

"What is she?"

"That information is not available."

"What about Stefan Dubois?"

"Stefan Dubois is not in our database."

"Why does Richard want the crucifix?"

"We cannot identify an association between Richard Kelly and the object crucifix."

Ciaran shook his head. "Why did Sciphil Two's troop tattoo a crucifix on my arm?"

"Negative. We do not have the record of them performing such task. You have three seconds left."

Three loud beeps were emitted by the computer, and the voice died out.

Silence.

Ciaran paced, contemplating the plans.

"This is so fucked up. So the grandfather deal wasn't bogus," Tadgh said.

"Ciaran, do you think the crucifix at Fountains Abbey is fake?" Jo asked.

Ciaran shook his head, still circling the room.

"You're make me dizzy, Ciaran. Say something," Tadgh said.

Ciaran deduced aloud. "All right, we have too much information about one thing and not enough of another. Let's tackle this one thing at a time. I think Richard Kelley, Madeline's grandfather, is onto something bigger than a crucifix. But I think the crucifix is real."

He pulled his left sleeve up and studied at the tattoo the robotic soldiers had inked him with at the creek. Jo and Tadgh looked at it, turned their heads sideways and upside down to look at it from all angles.

"It looks like a key from this angle," Jo said.

"Yeah!" Tadgh agreed.

"Key? To what?" Ciaran muttered the question to himself. His phone buzzed. On the screen, a line of text appeared, *"Your troops are ready at Henley on Thames. Specific locations will be indicated on maps."*

"Let's go." Ciaran said.

In the car, the device Ciaran had in his pocket buzzed. He pulled it out and gave it to Jo. "Okay, the bug in Madeline's pocket has received signals," she said and adjusted the speaker volume.

They heard voices at the other end.

"How much further have we got to go?" a male voice asked.

"Douglas, we've only scanned halfway and on one side. This isn't going to work," Stefan said.

"Then ask for more scanners and get them to do the scanning," Madeline said.

"Call Richard," Stefan commanded.

Stefan continued, "Ten more scanners . . . give me the phone . . . Mr. Kelley, if you were online this morning, you heard Ciaran. They've sniffed this site out. That means we can't stop now. Do you think he really went home to dance at a party? I need more men here to sweep the site fast. As many as possible. They have to be able to fight, if necessary. I don't know what sort of manpower Ciaran has access to. But we have to be prepared for the worst-case scenario if you don't want to lose the crucifix . . .

"How many can you spare?" Stefan laughed. "You've never been to this planet, have you? You can't send hundreds of your men here to run around civilian areas with guns and scanners and not alert the cops. I've already killed a cop, and Ciaran would turn me in to the police in a heartbeat. I need men strong enough to go against Ciaran but subtle enough to stay off the police radar . . .

"I'll take fifty. Ten on the ground and forty to back them up. Can you provide that?" Stefan asked. "I'll need to talk to them, but not here." Stefan seemed to finish his conversation with Richard. "Madeline," he said, "we need to go back to the villa . . . take . . . what's this?"

"I don't know," Madeline said.

"It's a bug. Douglas, do you know what this is? It was in her pocket."

Ciaran hit the brakes, and the car fishtailed as he swung to the side of the road and stopped. They heard struggling—and then static.

"Let go of my arm, Stefan," Madeline said.

"She bugged us. Probably sent signals straight to Ciaran. Give me that rope," Stefan said.

"Don't you dare, Stefan! Douglas, you work for my grandfather. If I lose a hair, you'll answer to him."

"Take your hand off her," a male voice said.

"Let go of me!" Madeline yelled.

"Weapons down. Put them away," the male voice commanded. "She's right, we don't work for you. Let's get back to the villa, and then we can work things out."

The signal died.

Ciaran stepped out of the car. He needed some fresh air. His world had stopped and started so many times in the last two minutes.

He couldn't make that mistake again. He couldn't let that happen to the woman he loved . . . again. Then it dawned on him that he'd never told Madeline he loved her.

He wasn't sure he was capable of delivering that emotion.

He inhaled deeply, scolding himself, then regained control of his temper and stepped back into the car.

# CHAPTER 24

The dusk was settling on the horizon when Ciaran and his troops got back to Fountains Abbey site. The soldiers came equipped with a lot of rope.

Ciaran spoke softly but firmly to the robotic soldiers. "I remind you again, only discharge your weapon if it is absolutely necessary. The best-case scenario is that we do not have to kill anyone. However, casualties might be unavoidable. Our opponents are dangerous, and they are trained to kill. I believe we will be outnumbered. Within the best of my capability, I promise to return you to your employer, as much as possible in the same condition that I received you. Am I understood?" They all nodded.

Ciaran spoke to James, the leader of the soldier group. "Can these soldiers perform advanced tasks?"

James shook his head. "Unfortunately not. But they're very stable and expendable."

"How long have you been working for these people?"

"Five years. I have enough experience, if that's what you're concerned about."

"No. I'm not concern about your experience. But we are going against robotic soldiers, and I don't care to have any human casualties."

"I signed up for it. It's the same at the other end. The commander is going to be human. They don't have robots that can carry out complicated tasks yet."

Ciaran nodded. "Is twenty the maximum number we can get."

James nodded. "For now."

"This morning, they scanned half of the right-hand side of the lake, looking down from the abbeys. So we'll set our people up on the left-hand side only. My prediction, however, is that the crucifix is not lakeside but somewhere in the abbeys. Thus, when they get there, I want only their key people left. By key people, I mean Madeline and Stefan. It might not be possible. But that's the best scenario."

James nodded.

"Focus on parts of the lake that have hillsides as close to the water as possible. Get your men up as high as they can go, and work in groups of three."

"Why?"

"Have you ever read Sun Tzu's *Art of War*?"

James shook his head.

Ciaran smiled. "You don't need to. You're practicing it now."

❊❊❊

At the villa outside of London where they had received the holocast of Richard Kelley, Madeline and Stefan stared blankly at a group of fifty men in heavy-duty military uniforms.

Stefan yelled, "Michael!"

Five soldiers stomped their feet in a military style and saluted.

"Yes, sir," they responded.

"Oh, yes. Dandy. Ten percent of our troop is called Michael." Stefan laughed. Then he grabbed the phone again. "Richard, on which planet are you living?"

"You wanted fifty men, I gave you fifty," Richard responded.

"I told you, I need soldiers that can fight. Not these meatballs."

The head of the fighter group, Douglas, looked angry at Stefan's comment.

Madeline knew they needed the fighters used at Robert's place — the flying and dart-throwing men. But she wasn't going to help Stefan get better men to fight against Ciaran. She just wanted Stefan to march in there and get the crucifix. Ideally, there would be no fighting.

"Let's get to work," Stefan said and pointed at Douglas. "You, with me." Then he stomped off.

Madeline saw the look on Douglas's face. *Keep that going, Stefan, and you'll catch a bullet very soon,* Madeline thought.

"The five of you with me this morning? You will be right behind Madeline and myself. We'll get ten men to do the scanning. The other forty will surround us from the outside. We'll be working our way from the lake up to the abbeys, as planned. My guess is that if they attack us, it will be lakeside. The abbeys are too confined for large numbers of men. So I want you five to stick with us, all the way to the abbeys. These meatballs? They're expendable. Got that?" Stefan commanded.

Douglas nodded coldly.

"The forty surrounding men, tell them to shoot at anything moving," Stefan directed.

"They were hired for you. Why don't *you* tell them? I only handle my four fighters," Douglas responded.

Stefan glared at Douglas. Then he nodded and walked toward the hired soldiers.

❄ ❄ ❄

Later at Fountains Abbey, Madeline looked at the site. Cold wind twisted between thousands of trees, making an eerie chanting sound. Despite the wind, the water in the lake looked calm—too calm, as if there were legions of ancient soldiers hiding underneath that would rise up and charge at them at any moment.

It was getting colder the later in the night it got. Ten of Stefan's soldiers were hunched down behind some small bushes. They needed to have a clear view of the lake and the team down there. They could see ten men with scanners, working slowly in a line on the left bank of the lake. Madeline and Stefan walked behind them, followed by the five fighters.

Except for the eerie sounds from the bush and the crackle of occasional movements from wild animals through the forested area, it was quiet and seemed as if there was nothing much to worry about.

At a distance, on much higher ground and far behind Stefan's men, were Ciaran's people. There were many trees around that blocked their view. However, Ciaran was certain that they had the ground covered.

He moved stealthily between the trees. He wanted to get closer to keep an eye on Madeline, but to do so, he would have to get rid of the first line of Stefan's men.

Ciaran signaled. His flashlight revealed a very small white dot. In the night, it looked like a reflection from an animal eye. He flashed three times.

A bird was released. It made a quacking sound and flew into the bush, flapping its wings and rustling leaves and tree branches.

A couple of men in Stefan's troop looked up. Seeing nothing, they focused once again on the team down at the lake. They did not realize that the last two men in their line had been taken when the bird distracted them.

From the back, Ciaran asked James, "How many men are down there?"

"Forty in the bush, ten scanning at the lake, and five walking with Madeline and Stefan."

Ciaran nodded. "Those five will be tough to get rid of. They're real fighters. And we don't have enough tranquilizers for the rest. So some of them will have to be taken down by force. How far along are they in the scanning of the lakeshore?"

"About twenty percent complete."

Ciaran contemplated. Then he said, "I'm changing the plan a bit. I need a direct path to get down there, and this line of ten has to be taken down quickly. We only got two of them, and they haven't figured they're missing guys yet. If you give me another three men from the north corner, I'll take down the remaining eight at once."

"Will do, right now," James responded and disappeared into the trees.

Stefan's eight remaining men were watching the team down by the lake. The last man looked behind him and found that the last two men in line were missing. He turned to alert the others. But before he could say anything, Ciaran's men released a cage full of bats. They flew straight into the group of soldiers. The men jumped, and some yelped.

Stefan looked up at the chaotic sounds coming from above the lake and saw soldiers dodging the bats. He rolled his eyes and said to Madeline, "Like I said, meatballs."

Madeline merely smiled and said nothing. She looked up and saw a white dot blinking three times. She smiled again and kept on walking.

While the men danced amid the cloud of bats, lines of rope dropped down at them and hoisted them up to the trees. Tranquilizers worked very efficiently, and the eight soldiers were quickly tied up, gagged, and put snugly to sleep among the small bushes.

Ciaran closed the gap and moved to a closer position. There, he could see Madeline clearly.

They were getting close to the temple. Ciaran wanted the next group of ten taken down as they were standing right behind it. He used his flashlight to signal again. A blue dot blinked three times in response.

Tadgh got Ciaran's signal. He was to take down the second line of ten men. He had three men, including himself. It would be four against ten.

Tadgh held two tranquilizer guns, one in each hand. The four men approached the line of ten from behind. On Tadgh's signal, they shot tranquilizers into five of the men. As soon as they were down, Tadgh charged forward, and with two kicks, he knocked the gun away from one of the soldiers. Tadgh's three other men threw ropes around the remaining soldiers' arms, effectively incapacitating their ability to shoot. They wanted to avoid any gun discharge as much as possible because they were still outnumbered by a large proportion.

Tadgh went one-on-one with the soldier and lost his gun. He took the soldier down very quickly. Looking around, he saw his men had restrained the other four. Tadgh said, "Let's just gag them and save the rest of the tranquilizers for the others." They secured the captured soldiers, and Tadgh signaled Ciaran.

Seeing Tadgh's signal, Ciaran smiled and moved down closer to the temple.

Ciaran could see the scanners had gone inside. He'd wanted that, however, the fighters were still behind Madeline and Stefan. He could see them approaching the temple.

Ciaran signaled.

Jo was at the far end with a remote control. As soon as she saw Ciaran's signal, she pressed a button. Smoke exploded from inside the temple just before Madeline and Stefan walked in. Five of the scanning soldiers collapsed, and the other five hurried outside.

Douglas darted to the temple. He looked inside, and when the smoke subsided, he stepped in.

Stefan looked around the hillside. He saw no one but his men.

Douglas exited the old building. "It wasn't a bomb. Just tranquilization," he reported.

Madeline smiled.

Stefan walked around. "So this is how he wants to play. Smoke people to sleep. I know he's up there. Where are my men? Go check on them."

Douglas raised an eyebrow. "Me? You want me to leave you?"

Stefan waved his hand absently. "No, you stay here. Send one of your fighters."

Douglas nodded and sent a man up the hill to check on the supporting soldiers.

Ciaran signaled Tadgh. Tadgh prepared his men. But when he looked back again, the fighter had disappeared.

# CHAPTER 25

Ciaran's view was blocked. He didn't see Tadgh's signal that he had lost sight of the fighter. It was way too quiet from Tadgh's direction. Ciaran moved a bit closer.

From the darkness, the fighter flew out with a forceful kick. Ciaran dropped his gun, fell, rolled down the hillside, and dropped onto the stone below. The fighter raised his gun to shoot at Ciaran.

Tadgh jumped out from behind the tree and kicked away the enemy's gun. The encounter was too close to use handguns, so they used their fists instead.

Tadgh was a skilled fighter and quickly dominated the fight as Ciaran climbed back up. With one last kick,

Tadgh sent the fighter down. He stayed down. Tadgh moved to grab him and restrain him, but the fighter suddenly swung at him with a knife.

Ciaran saw the flash of the blade, but it was too late for Tadgh. He ducked, but the knife still slashed through his side.

Tadgh was on the ground. Ciaran flew at the fighter and pounded him. He had to take the man quickly. He took the knife and restrained him. The man pulled out a dart, and Ciaran knew exactly what it was. With lightning speed, Ciaran's fist landed on the fighter's neck. There was a snapping sound, and the fighter went limp.

Ciaran ran forward, pulling Tadgh up. Tadgh puffed out the words, "No worries, just a flesh wound."

Jo rushed toward them. She touched Tadgh's side. "Jesus Christ, this is a lot of blood," Jo said.

"It's a flesh wound," Tadgh grumbled again.

"You're going back to the van," Ciaran said. "Jo, he's all yours. Please take him back to the van and do what you can to stop that bleeding."

Jo pulled Tadgh up, ignoring his protests.

❖ ❖ ❖

At the lake, the head of the fighters looked up the hill. "Fighter down," Douglas said dryly.

"What about the rest?" Stefan asked.

Douglas shrugged. "I don't know. They're your men. Who did you set to report?"

"I thought it was you," Stefan said.

"No, I told you, I only handle these men. I have one man down now, and I won't send more up there to get killed."

"Isn't it your job to protect us?" Stefan asked.

"No, we work for Richard Kelley. We're here to protect Madeline. He hired these soldiers for you. They won't listen to me."

"Son of a bitch," Stefan growled and grabbed Douglas's collar, barely moving him an inch.

"This is your first and the last warning. Take your hands off me," Douglas said.

Stefan released him.

"We should keep going," Madeline said. "If Ciaran has us surrounded, we need to keep these fighters with us to get to the crucifix and get out of here. There's no time for you to throw a tantrum."

"Throw a tantrum? I'll show you what it's like when I throw a tantrum."

Stefan grabbed Madeline at the back of her jacket and dragged her close to the edge of the lake. He held her in front of him to block any shots from the hillside.

Stefan yelled out, "Ciaran, I know you can see me. I want to play nice, but you're playing some psycho game with me. Ciaran!"

Silence.

"Ciaran!" Stefan yelled again. "If you don't come out, I'll put a bullet in her head. You hear me?" Stefan's voice bounced off the water, to the hillside, and through the trees. He could hear his echo clearly.

Silence.

Stefan fired into the air. The loud boom from the gun discharge tore through the darkness. Birds flew out from the trees, and some wild animals leaped from the bush.

Sounds came from a tree right in front of them. Ciaran stepped out. "You have to give me time to move from one place to another. I don't fly, Stefan."

Madeline could see disaster coming. She could smell the hot blood in Stefan's breath. And there stood Ciaran, alone, against ten armed soldiers, one of them a mad man who was holding her captive. She had done all this to prevent Ciaran from getting to the stupid crucifix, and she could not let him finish in this way.

"My grandfather won't be happy with this," Madeline spoke to Douglas. She could see him straining against Stefan when he grabbed her. But he was in the same boat with Ciaran because Stefan was using her as his human shield.

Madeline was angry. How many times had Stefan used her in this manner? What a coward.

"Let her go. As you can see, I'm unarmed, Stefan," Ciaran said.

Stefan laughed. "I don't think you're stupid enough to come here unarmed, Ciaran. How many of your men are up there? How many bombs did you plant down here?"

Madeline's body was pressed against Stefan's. She could hardly breathe. He held her so tightly and had his gun pressed right against her temple. Madeline thought if he didn't shoot her, the pressure from the gun would punch a hole in her head anyway.

"If you want to find the crucifix, go find it yourself. Why do you always hide behind women? First Juliette, and now Madeline," Ciaran said.

"I don't hide behind women!" Stefan screamed out the words and moved the gun to shoot at Ciaran.

Ciaran dodged. The bullet grazed his left arm.

When Stefan took the gun off her, Madeline tilted her head forward and then flipped it back as hard as she could, hitting Stefan on the nose. When he staggered, she turned around and shoved him full force into the lake.

Madeline ran toward Ciaran. He grabbed her hand, and they both took off into the bush, disappearing into the shadowy recesses among the trees.

❊ ❊ ❊

They ran. Ciaran helped Madeline climb the hills. He held her hand in his, and he could feel her energy, her breathing. On a stone platform behind the trees, when he was sure they were alone, he stopped, cupping her face. "Don't ever leave me again," he said. And he kissed her.

A few hours ago, he couldn't even think about how it would feel to have her in his arms again. And now, he would breathe her in if he could.

When they turned to leave, a fireball dropped to the ground near them. A couple of trees burst into flame. He protectively pushed Madeline behind him.

From the darkness behind some trees, four fighters jumped out.

Ciaran glanced up the hill and saw the shadows of his people closing in. But before they would be close enough to give him assistance, he had to handle these men.

They were good fighters and moved extremely fast. They knocked his gun from his hand and pounded on him. Two fighters kicked Ciaran at once. He fell on the ground and rolled away. His head hit the stone base behind, leaving him dazed.

Douglas pulled out his gun.

Madeline jumped in front of him. "Please, don't shoot. Please, for God's sake. I'm going with you."

Douglas thrust his gun forward. Madeline stood in front of the muzzle. "I'll go with you and get the crucifix. You will have all of my grandfather's praise and glory. Stefan is down there looking for the crucifix himself. If you shoot Ciaran, nobody will stop Stefan. Please, don't!"

Douglas did not hesitate for long. He grabbed Madeline and fled down the hill.

Ciaran tried to reach for her, but his vision was still blurry, and his body was not cooperating. Tadgh and Jo arrived. Tadgh pulled his brother to his feet.

"You should be in the van," Ciaran scolded.

"Look who's talking," Tadgh responded.

Ciaran kicked a tree in frustration and anger. "They took her again! I'll get the crucifix, and I'll get Madeline. Fuck them all!" Ciaran charged away toward his men.

Another fireball dropped down right in front of Ciaran. The bright flash of light revealed the positions of all the soldiers from both sides.

They were only meters from one another.

Stefan had told them to shoot at anything moving, so his soldiers pulled their guns, prepared for a massacre.

Ciaran yelled at his men, "Use your weapons! Fight!"

The two sides charged at one another. At that moment, they were even-numbered.

# CHAPTER 26

When Madeline and the fighters got down the hillside to level ground, Stefan had recovered the five soldiers who had done the scanning previously. They were waiting by the graveyard flanking the abbey. They had scanned quickly, working their way through the graveyard.

Madeline guessed they'd found nothing except the remains of dead bodies, both human and animal.

Stefan's nose was bleeding, and his clothes were soaking wet.

Douglas asked her, "What do you want to do? We don't have scanners. And I can't go back to Mr. Kelley with only you after losing so many of his men."

"We have to negotiate with Stefan then. You have the real fighters. Stefan will need them when he's up against Ciaran. I appreciate that you didn't shoot Ciaran. I'll make it up to you." Douglas nodded.

They headed up the hill toward the graveyard. Seeing Madeline, Stefan pulled his gun. "You bitch."

She just glared daringly at him, and the group of fighters pointed guns at him. Madeline cocked an eyebrow, waiting. Stefan was a smart man. He would work it out. Five of the so-called soldiers against the strong fighter group was not good odds.

"What do you want now?" Stefan asked.

"Same deal. They need me and a sample of the gold you'll find in the crucifix. So they still need you and your scanners. Ciaran and his men are coming down. All of your men up the hill are gone. You'll need these fighters or you won't get out of here alive. Your choice," Madeline responded.

"All of my men are gone?" Stefan asked Douglas.

"I could only manage to get her back. I can't protect your men. They didn't have any leadership up there. As a result, they were slaughtered."

He lied without a blink, Madeline thought. That had to work.

It did.

"Then dig in," Stefan said. "And don't be a fool. You won't get lucky again," he warned Madeline.

❊ ❊ ❊

Up on the hill, the fight had finished. Ciaran, Tadgh, and Jo were taking inventory. "I'm sorry, we've lost ten," Ciaran spoke to James.

James said firmly, "It was still a win. We took out twenty of them. There were ten more down the lake. But taking the fighters will not be easy."

Ciaran asked Tadgh, "How is your injury?"

"Do I need to say it? I'm alive and kicking. Told you it was just a flesh wound. But you'll have to fix Jo's dislocated shoulder." Tadgh gingerly led Jo to Ciaran.

"May I look?" Ciaran asked. Jo nodded.

Ciaran held her left arm up gently. Holding Jo's arm with his left hand, his right hand touching her shoulder lightly and very gently, he snapped it back.

Jo yelped in pain, and tears escaped from her eyes. Ciaran held her and kissed her forehead. "I know it hurt. I'm sorry. We'll get you a sling to wear, but for now, try not to move your shoulder too much." Jo nodded.

He handed her off to Tadgh and headed down the hill.

❀ ❀ ❀

Stefan led the way to the abbey via the courtyard. It had started to rain. They walked through the wet grass and muddy areas between the graveyard and the abbey. Madeline glanced up to the hill, knowing Ciaran and his people were up there. She knew he would come after her, and there was nothing she could do to prevent that.

As they entered the long courtyard, Stefan asked the fighters to come inside with him, and he left the soldiers at the entrance. They stayed there for a while and then entered to start the scan.

The rain came down even harder.

Madeline caught a smirk on Stefan's face.

*What's that about?* She'd seen the same thing at the hotel when he'd called Ciaran to tell him about her grandfather. That smirk. She couldn't figure out what it meant.

Then she looked outside.

Through rows and rows of stone columns and arched doorways, the view she had was of a dark and wet canvas and Ciaran's men approaching the abbey.

That very path was where Stefan had been lurking before he entered the hall.

It was not the rain and the thunder.

She had been mistaken.

An explosion tore through the air, the rain, and her heart. The men in front of her were blown into pieces.

"Ciaran!" she heard the scream in her head. Or maybe she screamed out loud.

There was no way anyone could have survived the explosion.

Madeline tore through the rain and the mud, sprinting outside. The wind slapped at her face. She couldn't hear much. Her ears were ringing with fear.

The world was empty. Dark. And quiet.

She would not believe that Ciaran was dead until she saw him for herself.

## CHAPTER 27

The explosion had left a deep hole in the ground. Despite the rain, there was fire and the acrid smell of burnt flesh. Body pieces were strewn about.

She walked into the middle of the massacre. But she refused to come to any conclusion until she found him.

She scrambled to each body, every body part, on all fours, swimming in the mixture of fresh blood, mud, and rain water.

She would search until she found something that belonged to him.

She kept looking. She didn't know for how long. She wouldn't give up until she had looked at everything she could find.

And then that was the end of it. She had seen everything. She felt like laughing. She was giddy.

She could not find his body or any evidence of it.

Douglas appeared beside her.

He didn't recognize the expression on her face. He must have thought she was grieving. *Keep it up*, Madeline told herself.

Douglas brought her inside. "I'm very sorry," he said.

*He thinks Ciaran is dead. Good. Let him think that.* Madeline maintained an expression to suit the scene.

They had completed the scanning inside the main hall of the abbey and found nothing. Madeline thought if those cold stone walls could laugh, they would be, watching the bunch of lunatics digging for gold.

The rain had stopped.

They moved out to the central courtyard where magnificent stone columns and arches had witnessed a thousand years of glory, destruction, life, death, and grieving. The roofs were in ruins here and there, cutting the expansive view of the sky into bits and pieces. Madeline thought she could hear monks chanting, but it might have been her imagination.

"I think I've got it," a soldier spoke up.

Stefan and Douglas charged toward a roofless stone tower. The scanner showed them a ten-inch rectangular box buried right in the middle of the tower. They could see through the material of the box.

The prominent shape of a fancy crucifix was prominently displayed.

There was also something in the box that looked like a piece of paper, perhaps a note or a letter of some sort.

This was it. The crucifix everyone had been searching for, lying underneath a roofless tower, surrounded by stone walls and arched gothic windows, and maybe even guarded by thousands of souls and spirits.

"Shovel," Stefan commanded in excitement.

The ground was soft in the roofless tower. Two soldiers came with shovels. In a short moment, the box was revealed. A metal box with a small lock.

The box looked so innocent, Madeline thought. It was like a girl's secret diary box where she would lock away all of her thoughts and dreams of the prince who one day would ride in on a white horse to rescue her from the tower. Who would think it could be rigged with a ton of explosives? But apparently, Stefan and the others were not fools. They had sniffed out such things before they even touched the box.

The box was lowered to the ground. Madeline could see blood in everyone's eyes.

The look of greed.

A soldier reached out for the box. Stefan immediately put a bullet, point blank, into his head. "Touch it and die," he warned.

The other soldiers moved back. Douglas signaled his fighters, still guarding outside. The fighters shot wire to the top of the tower and arches over the courtyard. In the blink of an eye, all three fighters hoisted themselves up, half flying and half walking on the walls like spiders.

They were coming at Stefan and the soldiers. The soldiers were confused. They weren't sure which side they were on, but they drew their weapons.

Stefan reached down for the box, but a hard kick from Douglas pushed him backward. He reached for his gun, but there wasn't enough time. Douglas pounded at him, releasing all of the hatred he had accumulated for him in the last day.

Madeline looked through the line of stone columns that arched across a strip of grass which led toward the stone frame for a missing gate.

A gate to heaven.

She smiled at it.

At the bottom of the large stone frame stood Ciaran. He smiled back. All she had to do now was make a run for him.

Everyone was fighting for the box and whatever treasures it might hold for them. She was unimportant at the moment. They wouldn't pay any attention to her. She backed against a wall, contemplating the shortest route to Ciaran.

She looked again. Ciaran no longer stood under the stone frame. She knew he was coming for her. She should run in that direction.

Madeline glanced around her again. Douglas was in a one-on-one fight with Stefan. Three fighters were struggling against four soldiers. The constraints of space between stonewalls, columns, and arched footpaths did not provide a free shooting range for anyone.

They had to fight and eye the box at the same time.

Madeline stepped backward once more and ran.

Douglas saw her. He called out. "Get the girl!"

The fighter shot up his hanging wire to the top window of the roofless tower, flying away from the fighting scene below.

Madeline ran. She zigzagged around the stone column as much as she could. She ran as fast as she could. Behind her was the fighter, coming down from the sky on his wire and running across the tops of the stone arches and walls like a spider. Madeline looked back and saw him. She ran faster, knowing she probably wouldn't escape.

The fighter was approaching her from behind, hoping to scoop her up by the waist. She ran faster.

But there were no more columns for her to dodge around. She kept running, and she could feel the pressure of the air behind her when the fighter approached. He touched her waist.

From inside the long abbey hallway, Ciaran charged out, standing right in front of Madeline's path, his gun pointing at the coming fighter. The fighter instantly pulled his wire up, managed to grab the back of Madeline's jacket.

In the blink of an eye, Madeline was off the ground, dangling below the fighter, who would not let go of her jacket. They dangled above Ciaran.

Ciaran turned and aimed for the fighter's arm that held fast to his wire. The pain startled the fighter, and he dropped Madeline. Ciaran ran forward and caught her. They both fell to the ground, rolling.

Ciaran smiled. "You're not going to leave me, either on the ground or in the air."

They stood up and saw the fighter's body dangling next to a stone window. It appeared that he had lost control of his wire and smashed his head against the rough edge of a broken stone.

Ciaran and Madeline were about to run off when they saw Tadgh and Jo approaching. They turned to the abbey hallway to leave from the inside. At the other side of the courtyard, it appeared that the fight continued. They ran to the end of the hall and could hear the fight right outside.

Then Douglas darted into the hall and blocked their exit.

"I can't let you go, Madeline," Douglas said.

Ciaran pushed Madeline behind him. "I'll talk to Richard Kelley if you let Madeline go." Douglas glanced at the fight in the courtyard. One of his fighters was losing to Stefan.

They would have to leave the hall by the gateway Douglas was blocking. Ciaran approached slowly, Madeline, Tadgh, and Jo behind him.

"You want the box, go get it. I'll talk to Mr. Kelley regarding Madeline. I promise. You spared me a bullet. I owe you. I'll keep my promise. If you let Stefan abscond with the box, he'll never come back. He doesn't keep promises," Ciaran said.

The fighter who was losing to Stefan pulled out a small explosive device.

Stefan knew what it was. It'd kill everyone in the confined space. He stopped pounding as the fighter picked up the box and threw it toward Douglas. At the same time, Stefan kicked the explosive device away and shot at the fighter.

Douglas dove through the air to catch the box. It was a good catch. He got it. On his landing, a bullet from Stefan's gun tore through air at him, striking him in the head. Douglas's body fell to the floor.

The box slid out from his hand, skidded on the ground, and stopped mere feet away from Ciaran.

Madeline tugged at him. "Get away! Get away from it! I won't let you touch it."

# CHAPTER 28

Ciaran turned around. "Don't worry. I know, Madeline." He held her hand so that they could move past Douglas's body to the exit.

Stefan charged to the hallway and stood at the exit. But he was focused on the box and nothing else. It was as if he didn't see anything. He pointed his gun at the lock on the box.

"No, you'll damage the crucifix," Madeline said. She didn't want to be here in case the box exploded.

Stefan looked at Madeline. He nodded his head and smiled strangely. He looked strange—so strange it made her worry about what he might do next. His eyes filled with a strange combination of satisfaction and confusion.

He looked like a vampire, starved for blood, but now that he had found the blood, he didn't know what to do with it.

They heard two loud bangs from outside. It appeared to be the end of the fight. They weren't sure who the victor was.

Then there was the slipping sound of the wired device, and the last fighter flew into the hall like a bird. He snatched the box off the ground, jumping on walls and stone columns so high that he almost hit the ceiling. He pulled himself up again to fly out of the hall via a gigantic window.

Stefan drew his gun and fired at him. The body of the fighter was carried by his wire, swinging outside via the window.

The box slipped from his hand and hit a stone arch on the ceiling. The lock was broken, and the lid swung open. The crucifix slid out, flipped a few rounds, and dropped on the floor with a thudding sound.

The top of the crucifix fell off, and the contents inside spilled out.

It looked like a black powder. The note from the box took its time, fluttering down and landing on the floor like a feather.

Stefan stood over the crucifix, walking around it as if he were a cat inspecting a dead rat, checking to be sure it was really dead.

He looked at Ciaran.

"It's certainly not gold," Stefan said with a strange smile on his face. He kneeled down to examine the strange powder.

Ciaran approached. Madeline pulled him back.

Stefan shoved both of his hands into the pile of black powder and let the grains run through his fingers. Then he let out a short laugh.

"It's dirt. I think it's dirt," Stefan said.

Stefan fingered the pile of dirt, rubbing some of it against his palms. He looked at his palms and laughed a little louder. "I think it's really dirt."

Madeline could not make sense of it. But Ciaran looked astonished, like he instantly knew what it meant as soon as the pile of dirt poured out from the crucifix.

Stefan picked up the note. He glanced at it then laughed some more. He held the note in Ciaran's direction.

"Recognize this handwriting?" Stefan asked. He read the note out loud, his eyes filled with amusement.

*"We came from dirt, we should return to dirt. I've made my choice of destiny. Please forgive and forget me. Consider that what you created was only dirt.*

*Your lost daughter and sister,*

*Juliette.*"

"She chose me," Ciaran mumbled to himself.

But Stefan heard him. "You're right. As usual, you're always right. You're her prince, she always said, her destiny."

Then Madeline got it. She understood now. It made perfect sense.

Guilt was the worst poison for Ciaran. Juliette had decided to betray her family for him. She was going to tell him. They were going to build a new life together. But she didn't have a chance to tell him any of that.

Madeline couldn't undo what Ciaran had seen and had heard. She knew it was better for him to live his life in doubt rather than knowing this naked truth. But it was too late.

Stefan sat on the floor, grinning like a lunatic.

Ciaran said nothing and did nothing. There was no movement from him at all.

Stefan said, between laughs, "She loved Ireland. She wanted a small cottage in the country. She wanted to be a teacher. How cliché was that? Dad always said she was too smart to do anything ordinary. You just do this one for Daddy, and then we'll set the family up for good. He always pushed her." Stefan began crying. "This big brother felt utterly stupid standing next to her. I couldn't do anything to help. She was nineteen. Met you when she was nineteen—and that was the end of her. I told Dad you were bad news. But he didn't listen to me. And now what? He's dead. She's dead. And all I have is this dirt! How is this fair?" Stefan screamed out the question again. "How is this fair?" while he pulled out his gun and shot at Ciaran.

It was too fast.

Ciaran didn't move, as if he was waiting for the bullet.

Tadgh was faster. He put a bullet in Stefan's head. Stefan's arm jerked, but he still managed to fire his gun.

The impact of the bullet pushed Ciaran a few steps backward, then he slumped to the floor.

Madeline grabbed at him. She knew it was bad. The bullet had hit Ciaran in his chest. Blood streamed from his wound and pooled on the cold floor.

She couldn't stop the blood.

Tadgh was calling for help and doing something else that Madeline didn't understand.

Madeline held Ciaran in her arms, hoping the sitting position would help lessen his blood loss. Ciaran's head lolled on her shoulder. She knew she was weeping. But she couldn't help it.

Ciaran shifted. "Let me see you," he said.

"Shhh, I've got you. Tadgh is getting help. Don't talk."

"Please," Ciaran asked again. His voice was so weak that it could hardly be heard.

Madeline lowered him to the floor. She took her jacket off to roll it under his head. Ciaran looked at her.

"I don't want to see you cry," Ciaran said.

She couldn't say anything. She just wept.

"I knew this day was coming. It's a debt I had to pay sooner or later. Had I made more progress in our relationship and then left you, it would be unfair to you. But if I didn't make any progress, it would be unfair to us. Before I go . . ."

"You're not going anywhere . . ."

"I love you, Madeline." He closed his eyes and didn't say anything more.

The room was filled with footsteps and people. Among these people, there was maybe Tadgh, Jo, Doctor Thomas. Madeline wasn't sure who said what. She just knew that Ciaran was no longer talking to her, or to anyone.

He just lay there silently in a pool of his own blood.

# CHAPTER 29

Jennifer was waiting when they wheeled Ciaran into the operating room. Doctor Thomas hooked up the machine to measure his vital signs.

Ciaran's pulse was extremely weak.

The medical team geared up quickly. No one followed the usual procedure of getting nonmedical personnel outside the room. Everyone stayed—Madeline, Tadgh, Jo, Jennifer, and even Migi.

In front of Madeline was a haze of noise and moving objects, none of which made any sense.

What made most sense to her now was that Doctor Thomas was performing some medical procedures and

Ciaran was going to be fine. Doctor Thomas was good at what he did.

He had once told Madeline that neither she nor Ciaran could take responsibility for other's people's actions. Juliette's death had not been Ciaran's fault, regardless of how he felt. She hoped he understood that.

Doctor Thomas held a syringe. *That must be anesthesia,* Madeline thought, knowing Ciaran would pay for it when he awoke. But he would just have to deal with it.

Ciaran seemed like he was saying something. Yes, he'd said something to Doctor Thomas, so soft that Doctor Thomas had to bend down to listen.

Doctor Thomas turned around. "Jennifer, he wants you." Doctor Thomas waved the medical staff outside the room.

Madeline was confused. Why would he do that?

Jennifer seemed to know what was going on. A wicked mom she was, Madeline thought. No worries. Madeline would wait for her turn to talk to Ciaran. Mothers come first. She understood.

Ciaran was so weak. He couldn't even open his eyes. Jennifer held his hand. She kissed it. She whispered something Madeline couldn't hear.

Ciaran forced his eyes open. Those beautiful gray eyes she knew and loved were now blurry with fatigue.

Ciaran looked up at his mother, and he said, "I'm sorry."

He kept looking at her.

Madeline was getting more confused. *Why did he keep looking at her?*

Then she realized he was no longer looking. His eyes had glassed over. His pulse had stopped, and her world had collapsed.

The monitor displayed a flat line.

Jennifer put his hand down. She closed his eyes and kissed his forehead.

Silence.

Then Tadgh grabbed Doctor Thomas. "Doctor, you have to do something. Can you resuscitate him? He lost a lot of blood, I . . . I know we have a rare blood type, but you can take mine."

Doctor Thomas shook his head. "He's gone, Tadgh."

"What do you mean? You haven't done anything! He hasn't tried, he can't just go . . ." Tadgh didn't realize he was weeping.

"I haven't told him I love him, Jo." Madeline grabbed her friend. "This is so unfair. He told me he loved me. But I didn't say anything. That wasn't right. I was stupid. I didn't respond . . ."

"Madeline, he understands. He's a smart man. Oh for God's sake, could you please cry? I'd rather you cry than look at me like that."

"Like what?" Then she realized her face was dry. There wasn't a tear in her eyes. Madeline's body started to shake, but she couldn't cry. She couldn't understand what was going on.

Tadgh grabbed at Doctor Thomas. "You're a *doctor*! You cure people! Please help him!"

"Tadgh, he was too weak to survive an operation, if he even wanted it."

"What do you mean?" Tadgh cried. "What do you mean? He didn't want it?"

"He knew his time was up, Tadgh. I loved him like my son. If I could have, don't you think I would have done something for him? You know that when Ciaran didn't want to fight, nobody could make him."

"Nobody?" Madeline's head poked up from Jo's shoulder. "Nobody?" Madeline repeated. "Look at him. He looks so peaceful. Wherever he is, he's enjoying this. He left us in this shit with all of our questions unanswered, with things he promised but didn't do, and he thinks he can get away with it? Everyone has to try. You have to try, Doctor Thomas. The LeBlancs make drugs. You save lives. How can this be so difficult?"

Jo pulled Madeline back when Madeline started to cry. She had started to realize the reality of the situation. But she wasn't sure if she would be able to accept it.

Jennifer stood silently next to Ciaran during the commotion in the room. Then she turned around and said, "May I have a moment with my family, please?"

Doctor Thomas, Jo, and Madeline left the room.

"Please stay, Madeline," Jennifer said, stopping Madeline in her tracks.

Madeline approached Jennifer.

There was not a single tear on the mother's face. Madeline felt pity for the woman. She felt pity for herself, too. She looked at Jennifer and waited.

"I believe you love my son, and he loves you."

Madeline nodded. What was the point of this, Madeline thought. Why did she use the present tense? *Loves*.

"Can you promise me that you would love and take care of Ciaran whenever you could manage it?"

Whenever she could manage it? Madeline didn't have to even promise to love him for the rest of her life? What was this woman doing? Madeline had just lost her true love, and Jennifer had lost her son. Madeline wanted to scream and leave this place. She wanted to grieve.

But now she was stuck here with this woman, feeling ridiculous.

Madeline realized she had never loved anyone before Ciaran. Yes, she'd had relationships with men, on and off, here and there.

But love is a sacred word, and if it used with the meaning it deserves, now was the time. It was for Ciaran.

"I'll always love him, whether he's dead or alive. But if you can bring him back, I'll be with him for the rest of my life, as long as he wants me. How's that for a promise?"

Tadgh approached. "Mother, what's going on?" he asked, the tears still damp on his face.

Jennifer held up a hand for silence. Then she pulled out a syringe with a golden liquid in it.

"Mother, what are you doing?"

Jennifer didn't answer. She checked the needle, and then she injected the liquid into a vein in Ciaran's neck.

Then she watched the monitor.

Nothing.

One moment.

Two moments.

Then the line jumped once.

And then again.

A line showing a healthy pulse ran across the monitor.

Jennifer nodded with satisfaction. "It's Ciaran's Golden Life. Apparently, it works."

Tadgh gasped. "Oh my God, oh Jesus Christ. You . . . you killed Juliette for this?"

"I didn't kill her. I wanted to teach her a lesson. I wanted their Golden Life to fail. I didn't know she was going to test the drug on herself. I swapped the drug. When I knew of the testing, it was too late."

Madeline was too stunned to speak.

"How will Ciaran live with this in his body?" Tadgh asked.

"It's up to you to tell him—or not. I'll lose him anyway, one way or another. But this way, I would lose him, but he would live." Jennifer looked at Tadgh and Madeline.

"If Ciaran were to never talk to me again for the rest of his life, I'd understand. I've never blamed anyone for this but myself." Jennifer opened the door and found Doctor Thomas waiting outside.

"Doctor Thomas, Ciaran's pulse is back. Could you please perform the operation now?" And with that, Jennifer walked away.

Doctor Thomas stormed into the room and looked at the monitor incredulously. He called out for his medical staff.

This time, everyone who was not on staff was sent from the room.

# CHAPTER 30

Madeline found Jennifer at the end of the hallway in the new quarter of Mon Ciel. Ciaran's mother looked as if she had aged twenty years since she had walked out of the operating room.

Madeline gave her a moment before she spoke. "I'll keep my promise, Jennifer. Thank you for bringing Ciaran back. I owe you my life."

Madeline gave Jennifer another moment to digest what she had just said. Then she hugged Jennifer.

Then and there, Jennifer cried.

The woman probably had not cried for years. Now, she probably felt old. She probably felt like a mother. Madeline held her for a long moment and let her weep.

When Jennifer's emotion subsided, Madeline asked, "Do you really want me to keep this information from Ciaran?"

Jennifer thought for a moment, then shook her head.

"He'll figure it out. I'd rather it come from you. I want you to add your perspective to the story when you tell him."

"Why me?"

"Because you love him like a soul mate. One day, I'd like to see you be the mother of his children."

"As far as I'm concerned, Juliette loved him, too."

Jennifer shook her head. "Have you ever considered leaving Ciaran if you knew your love could harm him?"

Madeline remembered it vividly. When she saw the number thirty-three written on the road and made the possible connection to her age, she had considered leaving him. She would have gone away with her grandfather if it would have spared Ciaran what just happened.

Madeline nodded.

Jennifer smiled. "If you love someone, you must be prepared to give, to take, and to let go. Out of the three, letting go is the hardest thing to do. Juliette never considered to letting anything go, no matter what it would do to Ciaran. You could argue that one might not understand the concept at twenty-one. But I'd venture to say it's in the nature of the person, not in their age or life experience."

Jennifer took Madeline's hand and continued. "I speak from personal experience. When you become a mother, you'll understand."

Jennifer put a small locket into Madeline's hand. "Juliette was his past. You are his future. As long as he can let his past go, he can have a future with you."

Jennifer turned on her heel and walked away as Madeline returned to the operation room.

❊ ❊ ❊

The familiar scent of his room welcomed Ciaran back to the world. Somehow, this world seemed better and much more pleasant than before. Because in spite of all the dark corners, rough edges, and puzzles life had presented to him, Madeline gave him one special thing, the feeling of being loved.

It felt good — being loved.

What happened at Fountains Abbey flooded back to him. But instead of the pain of regret, guilt, or sundry other dark patches of life, the memory was merely an event in a distant past.

It felt as if a lifetime of grieving had been lifted from him.

Even Juliette. He could think about her now with fond memories of the good times they had had together. He thought about her right now and recalled her brilliant smile and magnificent hair. He remembered the first time they met, and the smell of old paper in the library. The air around them had been so still that he had sworn he could hear her breathing. He remembered how happy she had been when she'd beaten him for the first time in a computer game. And he knew she was too smart not to know he'd let her win. But she'd enjoyed the victory anyway.

But those memories were now genuinely memories.

Previously, they had been mental scars, monuments for him to remember his sins, emotional crimes he had committed which destroyed innocence. A declaration of a lifetime debt to Juliette.

He remembered the sensation of the bullet penetrating his body. Was that it? His debt had been paid, and now he could move on?

Then Madeline entered the room like a fresh breeze in spring. She sat at his bedside.

"Hello!" she said.

"Hello back." He smiled at her. She was beautiful. He sat up, leaning against the headboard, and looked at her.

"Thank you," she said.

"For what?"

"For coming back to me. You wanted to go."

He smiled. "I changed my mind."

She tucked his hair back and kissed him. Then she eased back and looked into his eyes. "I love you, Ciaran."

"That's why I changed my mind. I've let go of whatever happened in the past. I'm hoping to have a future with you—if you'll accept me."

Tears rolled down her face. He wiped them away and rubbed his thumb at the dimple on her left cheek.

"Yes," she said. "Be with me."

He pulled her into his arms and felt the vibration of her emotion, of her love.

Over her shoulder, he saw a pot of Mountain Avens glaring at him from the corner of the room.

"What's with the flowers?" he asked.

She turned around, looking at the bunch of white flowers. "I found them in the back garden. I thought they were very pretty."

"They're Mountain Avens, Madeline."

"They have pretty name, too," she smiled.

"They were Juliette's favourite. This special kind doesn't grow here, so I brought them back from Ireland."

"Oh . . . so . . . do you want me to take them out?"

He smiled and lifted her chin up. "Why? You think they're pretty. You like them. That's what matters now."

They kissed each other.

There was jingle in the air, the merry kind. The flowers must have sung for joy because he let them stay in the room with his precious Madeline.

In the end, they were just flowers. But in a corner of his mind, a tune was playing. "Little hummingbird, do you see the sky? It is free. It is yours. Fly. Past the mountains. Past the oceans. There you will find love . . ."

He smiled to himself. *What a pretty song,* he thought.

This is the end of
Forever Mortal - A Shade of Mind - Book 2

THE NEXT BOOK
Elusive Beings - A Shade of Mind - Book 3
More information can be found at
Narrativeland.com/shade

# CHAPTER 1

.-.-.-.

The stench of fresh blood engulfed Madeline. She stormed into the living room of a country house in the middle of the Australian outback. With one hand still clinging to a fish basket and the other gripping a fishing spear, she approached the entrance of the adjacent reception room with caution.

She wanted to call out for Jo but thought that would be unwise.

It had been Jo's idea to travel all the way from New York for an exotic celebration of Jo's eighteenth birthday. Madeline hoped it didn't turn into the last trip of her life.

Madeline went out for the afternoon to take lessons from an Australian Aboriginal on how to catch fish the ancient way. They were going to have a surprise dinner for Jo tonight—a surprise because Jo disliked fish and Madeline didn't cook.

Luckily for them, the dinner was Zach's idea. He was their mutual Australian friend. Zach would turn twenty-one soon and planned to put the cozy kitchen of the small guest house to good use to celebrate a double birthday.

Blood.

It was all she could see in the reception room—amid the broken furniture.

Hesitating no more, Madeline yelled, "Jo!"

A cacophony of sounds—crashing glass, pots, pans, and other kitchen objects and a bloodcurdling scream—came in response, sending Madeline racing toward the kitchen.

More blood.

That was what she found. At the corner of the kitchen, Jo was on the floor, unconscious. Zach stood next to her, guarding her immobile body.

Zach's shirt was soaked in blood. He didn't look like he would be able to stand for long.

Larry, the host of the guest house, brandished a knife with one hand and held the other hand to his ear, screaming as if his head was going to explode. He reeled back and forth, crashing into the kitchen furniture and knocking it over.

There was no sign of his wife and children, but Madeline saw blood trailing out of the kitchen and through the door leading to the family room.

Larry was in his late sixties, a soft-spoken man and kind father and husband who had housed them for three days. That had been Larry before she'd finished her fishing lesson. But it wasn't the Larry before her now.

Zach was cornered. "Run, Madeline," Zach yelled.

She stood right at the door, not moving. She knew what was going on. "Is Jo alive?"

"Yes. Run, Madeline! He's insane. He's not listening, so don't even try to talk to him."

Larry directed his bloodshot eyes at Madeline. There was no humanity in him that she could see. The devil had taken over. An explicable smirk crossed his face as he approached her.

"Run, Madeline!" Zach yelled again and this time he captured Larry's attention. The old man swung his head back toward Zach.

Madeline threw the fish basket at Larry, hitting him in the head.

As soon as the basket left her hand she could smell it—the metallic stench from her ghost.

Larry turned to walk toward her, and Zach took the opportunity to charge him from behind. Larry suddenly swung back, and the knife in his hand slashed at Zach's abdomen. He grabbed Zach's neck with one hand and waved the knife with the other.

He was going to slaughter Zach.

Madeline knew Larry's strength was not his own. It was not his soul inside his body. "Larry, stop!" Madeline said firmly.

He released Zach instantly, dropping him to the floor unconscious to lie next to Jo. Then he turned to Madeline. Smirking, he walked toward her like a zombie. He didn't even threaten her with the knife to give her an excuse to kill him in self-defense. He simply staggered toward her with a crazed smile on his face.

In his eyes, she could still see the pledge of the kind old man who had been their friend for the last three days. She knew he was innocent.

He must have been the one who killed his wife and kids. But his body was only doing what it was being told to do.

The metallic stench of her ghost grew stronger. It was not the first time the ghost had possessed men to kill. All she had to do to end all this was to kill the man in front of her.

Once and for all, it would end.

But the old man was innocent.

She had never been able to do that, to end it, and the ghost kept coming back. Disaster after disaster. And people would continue to be murdered until she killed the host the ghost possessed.

Larry continued to approach Madeline.

"Don't come any closer." She stepped back.

Larry kept coming. She could see his eyes had started to clear. Once that happened, he would return to normal and see what he'd just done. Most often, the men, after being possessed, went insane and eventually killed themselves.

"Your last chance, Madeline. Keep your virtuous soul, and more people will die," an ancient voice echoed in the air.

She had to kill this innocent man for the craziness to end. The ghost had been telling her that for years—it would continue to kill until she killed an innocent man. But no matter how she tried to justify it, in front of her was a helpless man whom she had no right to kill.

Larry took another step toward her.

"Time is running out, Madeline. Next time, it will be worse," the ghost chanted.

"Stop, Larry!"

She yelled at the old man, but he kept advancing. She raised the fishing spear, pointing it at his heart.

# CHAPTER 2

.-.-.-.

*Ten years later.*

It was after six in the morning, but Madeline couldn't find any sign of the winter sun. She overanalyzed the humidity, the feel of the air, and the sound of the wind, concluding that England winters and New York winters were the same—cold and bleak.

Ciaran turned away from the window and looked at her.

Madeline should have gotten used to the sight of Ciaran by now, but it never happened. God must have been in a very good mood indeed when he created such a gorgeous human being. She could hardly believe that every inch of that six foot three slender yet muscular warrior's body belonged to her. His face—that of a dark angel—continued to make her stomach quiver. Those deep and intense gray eyes focused on her as if for him no one else existed and nothing else in the world mattered.

Suddenly a bullet hit Ciaran's chest, exiting from his back. Blood splattered onto the glass window. Madeline gasped as the image of Ciaran flickered and disappeared.

She shook her head and snapped back to reality. A few days ago, her life had changed forever.

She still remembered the sensation of Ciaran's blood on her hands, the commotion in the operation room, and the emptiness when she thought her world would exist without him in it.

She couldn't get the memory of his beautiful eyes, glassed over and lifeless, out of her mind. And she couldn't ignore the lingering fear that she would have to experience that incident again in the future. Ciaran said he had left the memory behind to move on with life, to be with her. But that was before she told him the truth behind his recovery.

It wasn't a miracle that he was back with her again.

Jennifer had wanted her to tell Ciaran, and she had. But regardless of how much she tried to spin the story and make it golden, the naked truth was that his mother had swapped the drug. And, as a result, Juliette had died, and the real drug had coincidentally saved his life.

Jennifer had told her that Juliette never let go of anything, and Madeline wagered she would cling to Ciaran this time more than at any other time.

This ordeal wasn't over yet. Not by a long shot.

The air seemed to thicken a bit. Madeline spun around, surveying the empty room around her. She didn't care for what she was feeling. This wasn't her familiar psychic blue dots. It wasn't the appearance of Juliette's hologram, either.

It was the unmistakable metallic stench of her long forgotten ghost. *Who was it going to possess now?* Fear rose in her mind like tidal waves.

"Madeline!"

Madeline startled and cried out.

"Are you okay?" Tadgh said from the door. "I knocked." Tadgh stood, puzzled, his hands in his pockets.

"Huh?"

"Can I have a word with you?"

"Of course." Madeline smiled. "Where's Jo?"

"Planning a new game in the game room . . ."

Madeline was a bit disturbed by Tadgh's apparent agitation as he rolled up and down on the balls of his feet. "What's up Tadgh?" she asked.

"I don't know. Something feels strange."

"Why wouldn't it seem that way, especially after all that's happened?"

"I called Dublin. They said Mother hasn't arrived home yet. She left ages ago. Where could she be?"

"Is there anywhere she might go to take some time off? Be by herself? She's been through a lot lately. What about your cousin George's in France? Jennifer mentioned him before."

Tadgh shook his head. "You don't know my mother. She's an authoritative figure in the family. She would never take shelter anywhere or protection from anyone—no matter how mad Ciaran might be at her. I even searched for air traffic info just in case . . ."

"There might have been an accident?"

Tadgh nodded. "Air, road, water . . . I looked everywhere. I even rang George, although I knew it was entirely unlikely that she'd gone to France. I couldn't find a hint of her. What did she say to you?"

"Nothing. She just cried."

"Do you . . ." Tadgh cleared his throat, "Do you think Mother did the right thing, you know, regarding Juliette?"

"I won't judge her, Tadgh. One day, I will be a mother, too, and I don't know what I would do or what I will be capable of when it comes to the welfare of my own children."

Tadgh nodded.

"Let me see what I can do," Madeline said and closed her eyes. She tried to catch a sense of Jennifer's mind—a trace, a feel, a hint of even a single blue dot somewhere.

A dot suddenly appeared at the back of her mind, quickly expanding and exploding like a bomb, spraying dark blood particles all over her. The metallic stench engulfed her senses.

Madeline yelped and slumped to the floor.

"Madeline, are you okay?" Tadgh ran to her, holding her by the shoulders and sitting her up.

"Do you smell anything strange in the room, Tadgh?"

He squinted his nose, sniffed, then shook his head. "Why? What's going on?"

She shook her head. "I can't see your mother, Tadgh."

"That's okay."

"I'll keep looking," Madeline promised.

"Where's Ciaran?" Tadgh asked.

Madeline smiled. "He said he was going out for some fresh air . . ." Her voice trailed off. She could swear that she had just seen the white Mountain Avens flowers she'd picked this morning bleeding. She'd watched as a drop of blood formed at the center of a single flower, rolled down a white petal, and landed on the table. She blinked, looking again closely.

Ciaran had said this was Juliette's favorite kind of flower, and he'd had them brought here from Ireland.

Tadgh frowned. "Are you okay, Madeline? Tell me what's going on."

"What color are those flowers over there, Tadgh?"

"They're white. Why do you ask?"

"Was Juliette by any chance buried near here?"

Tadgh cocked an eyebrow. "You want to buy her flowers?"

"Was she cremated or buried?"

"She was buried. The family's cemetery is nearby. Why?"

She wondered whether her ghost was able to possess an already dead body. Her mind's eye kept seeing the Mountain Avens dropping blood onto the table—it seems like an omen or a warning to her. She closed her eyes, concentrated, and traced Ciaran's thoughts.

Madeline muttered. "Ciaran is at the cemetery at the moment. Trouble's coming. I can feel it. He didn't bring his cell with him. We have to go there right away."

"Can't you channel to him, talk to him in your mind? You know, using your psychic trick."

"It's not a trick, Tadgh, it's an ability. And yes, I can channel and try to communicate with Ciaran. But he's not a psychic—he can't hear me and can't respond."

"Okay. Let's go then. Hope it's not too late. What's he thinking, not bringing his cell with him?"

"Nostalgia," Madeline muttered.

Tadgh led the way, and they rushed out of the room.

# CHAPTER 3

.-.-.-.

The bleak morning couldn't possibly weigh down the air at the cemetery any further than it already was. Rows and rows of graves lined up neatly in the grass. Even in death, the LeBlancs protected their privacy, and their private family plots were located at the far corner of the cemetery. Ciaran squinted at the sight of Tadgh and Madeline racing toward the tomb.

It started to drizzle.

Madeline rushed into the tomb and glanced around. She looked nervous—and she should be. He had managed to drag her into the tangled mess of his past in no time. He pulled Madeline into his arms as soon as she ran inside, holding her tightly until every muscle in his body quivered with emotion. In the corner, Tadgh shook rainwater from his coat.

Suddenly, the air thickened. Ciaran knew what it was, and he didn't care for it one bit.

It meant trouble.

"Tadgh, get out of here. Now!" Ciaran called out to his brother.

As the candle in the tomb flickered, and the faint but sharp smell of burning electrical current rushed through the room, a hologram of Juliette appeared. Ciaran wasn't at all surprised to see it—someone had simulated her image, and he had seen it in the hologame.

But he was stunned at how the raw emotion flooded back to him, seeing her this close and this real again.

She wore a red dress and stood next to the altar, smiling graciously at him.

"You killed my brother, Ciaran."

"He nearly killed me, too." Ciaran moved Madeline behind him protectively, almost squashing her against the wall.

"Yes, you're right. You told me that before. But in battle, someone always gets hurt."

"What do you want, whoever you are?"

"I'm Juliette," she said. *"Your* Juliette. Or I was once. I died on Earth because of you. My father traded his life to get me out of here. And now you've killed my brother. So it's only fair to ask you to come back to me, isn't it? All you have to do is to go through the gate."

"What gate?"

"The Daimon Gate. All of the information you need is on the disk I hid at Mon Ciel. Process the disk, and then you'll be able to see the gate. Come here and be with me."

"I don't have the disk."

Juliette nodded. "Oh, it's that old man Richard again, isn't it? He got the disk, didn't he? But he won't know how to decode it. Not everyone is as smart as you and me, Ciaran. You need to find the disk and decode it." She smiled again. "I miss you."

"And what if he won't go through the gate?" Madeline asked.

Juliette laughed. "Oh, sister. Of course, you'd ask such a foolish question. You do think you have a claim on my man."

The holographic Juliette cast an evil eye at Madeline. Ciaran moved forward slightly.

"You're no competition for Madeline," Ciaran told the hologram. "You can't compare yourself with the innocent Juliette I loved years ago. You're an electronic profile. Nothing more. Juliette died. You might be able to simulate her emotions and experiences, but you can't simulate the real love we had for each other."

"I *am* your Juliette! I didn't die!" The hologram whirled back and forth. Its skin grew radiant and red.

"You just told me that you died on Earth because of me. That was a lie?"

"No. I did die on Earth. But I live elsewhere now. You have to be with me. You have to go through the gate."

Tadgh sneered. "So you're in hell now? I would say heaven, but given what you did, I wouldn't think heaven would take you."

"Tadgh!" Ciaran warned him. He didn't want to make the hologram angry. He had a feeling it wasn't just a simple hologram with familiar properties. This hologram was something more, something new and more tangible. It might be able to do some real damage.

Tadgh continued. "As far as I'm concerned, Stefan shot my brother, and he got a bullet in return. That's a tit for a tat. You see, in battle, as you said, someone always gets hurt. If you had told Ciaran your motives from the beginning, you would never have been in a relationship with him, let alone in love and married. You cheated first. Unfortunately—like brother, like sister—you paid a consequence. I can't see that my brother owes you anything. We're done here."

"Tadgh is right. I owe you nothing, Juliette. Let me have my fond memories of you—and you stay wherever you are. I can't—I won't—join you." He tried to be firm, but Ciaran knew it wasn't going to work.

He pushed Madeline toward the door. The burned smell in the air thickened and grew stronger. They heard the faint sound of crackling wires and dry wood burning. "No one walks away from me." Juliette's face turned dark red, and then purple. "Including you." Her eyes filled with rage. "I won't allow it!"

Ciaran grabbed Madeline and called out for Tadgh, "Run!"

Madeline and Ciaran charged out of the tomb.

The hologram whirled and spun. The light circle around it extended until it became a gigantic cylinder.

It grew larger by the second, turning into a small tornado. It stirred the air and sucked everything loose inside the tomb into its vortex. It spun objects around and ejected them randomly in different directions.

It lifted a tombstone and threw it to the ground, breaking it into pieces. It unearthed a coffin and spun the lid away into the air. The tornado grew and exploded the tomb. Shards of rock and concrete rained down on the cemetery grounds.

Madeline, Ciaran, and Tadgh ran. They heard the explosion behind them, but they did not look back.

The tornado built up size and speed quickly. It rose into the darkening sky.

It grew. It chased.

Ciaran looked back and could see the tornado's need to devour. It would indiscriminately suck everyone and everything into it. But he knew its quest—it wanted only him.

*For a limited time, D.N. Leo gives away*
*4 books (e-version) in the Multiverse Collection*

**CLAIM YOUR BOOKS**
*http://narrativeland.com*

**THANK YOU FOR READING!**
**D.N. LEO**

## Random Psychic

## *A Shade of Mind Series*
### *Www.narrativeland.com/shade*

*1-4 Random Psychic*
*2-4 Forever Mortal*
*3-4 Elusive Beings*
*4-4 Imperfect Divine*

# D.N. LEO 'S NOVELS
# SERIES READING ORDER

http://www.narrativeland.com/dnleo-series-reading-order

## A SHADE OF MIND
(narrativeland.com/shade)
### *The Journey from Earth to Eudaiz*
Main Characters: Ciaran, Madeline, Tadgh, and Jo
(Recommended reading in order)
1-4 Random Psychic
2-4 Forever Mortal
3-4 Elusive Beings
4-4 Imperfect Divine

—

## SPECTRUM
(narrativeland.com/spectrum)
Main characters: Lorcan, Orla, Roy and Mori
(Recommended reading in order)
1-4 White Curse
2-4 Blue Fox
3-4 Indigo Stone
4-4 Red Moon

—

## MINDSCAPE
(narrativeland.com/mind)
Main characters:
Ciaran, Madeline, Tadgh, Jo, Kyle, Hoyt, Ayana, Pete,
Sizx, Lorcan, Orla
(Recommended reading in order within series, can be
read in ANY order in related to other series)

1-6 Queen's Gambit
2.- Knight & Pawn
3-6 Lone Castle
4-6 Doubled Bishops
5-6 Dead Squares
6-6 King's Endgame

—

## SILVER BLOOD

Main characters:
(narrativeland.com/silver)
Ciaran, Madeline, Tadgh, Jo, Caedmon, Sedna, Roy, Mori, Zach, Mya, Lorcan and Orla
This series can be read in ANY order within the series and in related to other series.

Virgo
Libra
Scorpio
Taurus
Pisces
Gemini

Thank you for reading.

If you enjoyed reading **Forever Mortal**, I would appreciate it if you would help others enjoy this book, too.

**Recommend it.** Please help other readers find this book by recommending it to friends, readers' groups and discussion boards.

**Review it.** Please tell other readers why you liked this book by reviewing it. A few sentences will make a significant difference to me. If you do write a review, please send me an email at info@dnleo.com so I can thank you with a personal email.

Connect with me online:
Web: narrativeland.com; Twitter: @dnleostory

To join my mailing list, please click here

Facebook page of the Outlanders of the Multiverse series
https://www.facebook.com/Outlandersofthemultiverse

# COPYRIGHT

## FOREVER MORTAL
A Shade of Mind - Book 2

## By D.N. Leo